## "Afraid to me for me, Jonathan?"

What on earth had made her ask that? That wasn't what she wanted to say to him at all.

He replied angrily, "Cut it out, Rosemary. I'm trying to set the record straight, that's all. I've enjoyed being with you. And I admit my original idea was to...."

"Get me into bed?" Her head tilted defiantly.

"Right. You've got it," Jonathan said harshly. "But I'm glad you had the sense to stop me the other night, because I've no right to use you ... when I can't give you anything in return."

Rosemary turned her head so that he couldn't see the sudden desolation in her eyes.

"You needn't worry," she lied to him. "Because you don't have anything to give me that I want."

**KAY GREGORY** is married, lives in Canada and has two grown-up sons. She recently began writing for Harlequin, and readers will welcome her latest novel in the Harlequin Romance line.

## Books by Kay Gregory

HARLEQUIN ROMANCE
2919—A STAR FOR A RING

# A PERFECT BEAST

## Kay Gregory

*Harlequin Books*

TORONTO • NEW YORK • LONDON
AMSTERDAM • PARIS • SYDNEY • HAMBURG
STOCKHOLM • ATHENS • TOKYO • MILAN

Original hardcover edition published in 1988
by Mills & Boon Limited

ISBN 0-373-03016-9

Harlequin Romance first edition November 1989

To my husband Bob,
and my mother Lorna,
who always said I should write a book,
and to Basil Jackson,
without whose inspiration
I never would have done it.

# CHAPTER ONE

'HOLD your fire. I surrender,' cried Henry apprehensively, ducking his ginger-coloured head to avoid the missile which came flying past his nose.

'Oh, Henry, I'm sorry.' Rosemary laughed and moved across the classroom to retrieve the broken pieces of chalk which lay scattered in powdery heaps against the fish tanks.

'No problem. I'm used to being a target. Maths isn't everyone's favourite subject.' Henry's small mouth parted in a puckish grin, and his bright blue eyes twinkled at her above chubby, rounded cheeks.

'No, I don't suppose it is. Do your students really use you for target practice?' Rosemary was intrigued.

'No.' He put his head thoughtfully on one side. 'And I don't think I'd allow it. I was merely trying to lighten that positively vicious expression on your usually charming face.'

'Oh, dear. Was it as bad as that?'

'Worse. What's eating our unflappable Miss Reid today? By the way, is your car still on the sick list? Want a ride home?'

'No, it's fixed, thanks. And don't worry about me. I'm not quite homicidal—yet.'

Henry's eyes widened in feigned alarm. 'Are you likely to be?'

'Quite probably if I have another day like this one.'

Rosemary ran her fingers distractedly through her long, pale-blonde hair, and discovered she was still clasping the chalk.

'Oh, no,' she groaned, as white flakes drifted on to her shoulders.

Henry laughed. 'The end of what was obviously a perfect day. Now you'll have to wash your hair, too.'

'Mm.' Rosemary nodded glumly. 'I will, won't I?'

'What's the matter, Rosemary? Anything very drastic?' Henry's kindly eyes registered concern.

'Oh, no, not really. Just an accumulation of minor irritations. You know, half the kids arriving late with wonderful excuses that you can't possibly prove are sheer imagination, six interruptions on the intercom in the first period, no replacement light-bulb for the slide projector, two of my best students handing incomplete work, the usual trouble with Colin Williams and Janey Thatcher trying to make out behind the gerbil cages, and now I've discovered that Tamsin Riordan has left her microscope out for the second day in a row.'

'Poor Miss Reid,' sympathised Henry.

'And to top it all off, I've just remembered I've got parents,' Rosemary finished dramatically. 'That's when I threw the chalk.' She tossed her hair behind her shoulders and smiled a little defensively, almost challenging Henry to suggest that her actions were anything less than reasonable.

He blinked. 'Most people have,' he said doubtfully. 'Have you only just discovered yours?'

Rosemary laughed and relaxed. 'Parents, you mean? No, I wasn't talking about my family in Kelowna. I meant I've got parents coming to see me about their darling children.'

'*Are* they darling children?'

'Probably. It's usually the parents we *don't* need to see who come, isn't it?' She pulled a piece of paper from the pocket of her lab coat, glanced at it, and groaned. 'I spoke too soon. I'm seeing Heather Fong's mother, which is no problem at all—and Tamsin Riordan's father.'

'He is a problem?'

'I've no idea, but his wretched daughter is.'

'Tamsin? Yes, I've got her, too. She's a bright enough kid, with a terminal allergy to work, I think. She just can't seem to apply herself.'

'Won't, you mean.'

'I'm not so sure. Let me know how you get on with the father.'

'I will. Thanks, Henry.' Rosemary smiled at him again and he thought what a difference it made to her serious little face. When she smiled, the faint freckles which dotted her cheekbones seemed to form laugh lines to her gold-flecked eyes, and the long, curving mouth curled infectiously at the corners.

Henry smiled back. 'See you tomorrow,' he said. 'Don't let the parents get you.'

Rosemary didn't intend to. She had not been exaggerating when she told Henry it had been a bad day, but somehow the sight of Henry's cheerful face poking round her door had done a lot to relieve her feelings and improve her temper. She would deal with Mrs Fong and Mr Riordan in her usual calm, friendly fashion, then she would go home, have a hot bath and retire to bed with a book.

She aimed the remainder of the chalk at a wastepaper basket, missed, and bent to pick it up. Then she sighed, and leaned her head wearily against a cabinet full of dissecting instruments. Of course she was bound to find things different now that she had transferred to this large, modern school in Vancouver. The school where she had taught for six years in Kelowna had been much smaller than Mathieson High, and it had taken a couple of months for her to adjust to the new, big-city environment. But until today she had felt she was getting along quite well. The students and staff seemed to like her, and Henry Parkinson's unfailing good nature had been a great source of comfort and support. And in spite of today she felt the move had been good for her, and the best possible way to achieve the change she so badly needed after the final break with Ronald.

Rosemary straightened her shoulders. She was not going to let one bad day get her down. Lifting her chin determinedly, she marched into her small, cluttered office at the back of the biology lab, pushed several heavy books to the back of her desk and, pulling a stack of lab reports towards her, began to mark homework.

She was so absorbed in her task that it was some time before she became aware of a scraping noise outside the door of her office. She glanced at her watch. Mr Riordan was not due until four thirty—almost fifteen minutes to go. But perhaps he was early. Reluctantly she put down her pen, stood up and walked into the outer lab.

Then she froze.

At the back of the room a pair of very broad shoulders in what looked like Harris tweed were bending over a cage. The lid of the cage was pushed back and a large hand was reaching down to touch the smooth skin of the iguana crouched watchfully at the bottom.

Rosemary took a deep breath. 'And just what do you think you're doing?' she asked, in a voice from which the usual lilting quality was noticeably absent.

The figure looming over the cage turned slowly, and Rosemary gasped.

He was very tall, with long arms and a powerful neck. His large head was bent slightly towards her, and she felt a sudden heat in the pit of her stomach, as though she had been singed by the smoke-grey eyes fixed so penetratingly on her face. Yet he was studying her quite dispassionately, from under heavy, well-shaped brows which were in dark contrast to the waving fairness of his tawny-blond hair. From his eyes, Rosemary's stunned gaze passed slowly to his mouth. It was a startlingly virile mouth, firm, full-lipped, and chiselled in that warm, sensual way that made women . . .

No. Now, wait a minute—what in the world was she thinking of? She had just caught this man messing about with her unpredictable iguana, and his rampant masculinity had nothing to do with anything. Had it?

He was watching her silently, leaning casually against the iguana cage. Rosemary swallowed, inhaled deeply, and began again.

'I asked what you were doing with my iguana?'

His unnerving grey eyes continued to stare at her thoughtfully. After what seemed like a very long time he replied in a deep, almost husky voice that played further havoc with Rosemary's stomach, 'I'm not doing anything with it. What's the problem?'

Rosemary's knuckles clenched white on the edge of the nearest lab table. Then she took a firm grip on herself and explained in as calm a voice as she could muster,

'The problem is mostly that iguanas have claws—and teeth, in case you hadn't noticed.'

'So?' The dark eyebrows rose in deliberately blank enquiry.

'So if you don't want to get hurt, you would be well advised to leave that little monster alone,' snapped Rosemary with unnecessary heat. This man was having a very odd effect on her.

'Would I?' The eyebrows returned to their rightful position as his eyes ran quickly around the classroom. He's probably taking in Tamsin's neglected microscope and all the things I haven't had time to put away, thought Rosemary resentfully. 'You most certainly would,' she said firmly. 'Look what he did to me.' She held out her arm to display a fading pink scar which stretched from the inside of her wrist to her elbow joint.

'Hm,' he said, moving towards her and casually lifting her hand to get a better look. 'I see what you mean.'

'Yes,' murmured Rosemary, who was suddenly finding it hard to breathe, 'so you must realise . . .'

'As a matter of fact, Miss Reid,' he said without inflection, 'what I realise is that you appear to have a dangerous animal loose in a class full of thoughtless adolescents. Not very responsible, is it?'

He was still holding her hand, and Rosemary pulled it furiously away. How dared this overwhelming man come barging into her classroom, start interfering with her iguana, and then have the nerve to accuse her of being irresponsible?

'The organisation of my classroom is my business, thank you,' she said tightly. 'But since you find it neccesary to ask, I am not a complete idiot. I don't know who you are, but . . .'

'I'm the father of one of your pupils.'

Rosemary closed her eyes. Of course. She should have known immediately that this man belonged to the one student who had so far caused her more concern than any other since moving to Mathieson High.

'Very well,' she continued resolutely. 'As I said, I am not a complete idiot. That cage is usually locked while the students are here. It's open now because I intend to clean it before I leave. And for your information, most of those "thoughtless adolescents" have a great deal more sense than some adults I could mention. They're biology students and have a healthy respect for the creatures they're here to study.'

'Which I haven't?' She saw a sudden spark flare in his eyes, making him look older and more formidable than before.

But Rosemary was not to be intimidated. She took a quick step backwards and locked her arms securely behind her. 'Apparently not,' she replied evenly.

When she saw his lips twist slightly, she became aware that she was talking to this large, obviously adult male as if he were a very small boy who had misbehaved, and suddenly she felt foolish—as if she herself were a little girl caught cheeking her elders. Then his much-too-sensitive mouth tightened, almost imperceptibly, as if he wanted to laugh but was determined to resist the temptation.

Rosemary decided the battle of the iguana had gone far enough. It was time to get this conversation back on track.

'You don't look much like Mrs Fong,' she began

gloomily, voicing her thoughts aloud.

'I'm glad,' he remarked drily.

'So I suppose you must be Mr Riordan,' she continued, ignoring the interruption. 'Do sit down.' She waved a hand at a stool in front of one of the tables, and perched herself uneasily on another which had the advantage of leaving several tables between herself and Tamsin's father—who ignored the stool she had indicated and seated himself unnecessarily close to Rosemary, so that when he extended his long legs and leaned back against the table, his knees brushed momentarily against hers. He smiled, his eyes fixed steadily on her face, and moved his legs to the left.

Rosemary swallowed. 'What would you like to discuss, Mr Riordan?' she asked, in the tight, clipped voice she adopted when she wanted to sound competent and efficient to disapproving parents who thought she was too young to teach their teenage children. At twenty-eight she still looked young for her age, and sometimes it was difficult to convince people that she was entirely capable of controlling a class of unruly adolescents.

The man's hypnotic grey eyes were now regarding her with a mixture of irritation—and something else. Amusement almost, and a sort of puzzled speculation.

'I would like to discuss my daughter's marks, for one thing,' he replied equably. 'And the fact that she feels you go out of your way to make things hard for her. Is that true, Miss Reid?'

'I go out of my way to make her work, if that's what you mean,' snapped Rosemary—and was immediately furious with herself for letting this interview get out of hand so quickly. Usually she got on well with parents and was able to smooth over any problems or misunderstandings. But not this time. Not with Tamsin's father. For some reason he made her react defensively, as if she were the one in the wrong.

He was watching her closely. 'Tamsin has always worked hard,' he said coolly. 'She has no problems with her other classes. Are you sure you have enough experience to handle the bright ones like my daughter?'

Rosemary took a deep breath. 'Mr Riordan,' she began, in a voice which started out brisk and capable and ended up raised in barely controlled anger, 'Mr Riordan, I have been teaching for six years, my reputation with students and parents has always been good. I have, of course, had difficult pupils, and more often than not we have been able to work together to solve their problems. But as I *am* human, there have naturally been failures, too. Perhaps sometimes the fault has been mine, although I hope not. But one thing I can say for sure, in all my years of teaching . . .'

'All six?' he queried mildly, raising an attractively enquiring eyebrow.

Rosemary glared at him, and forbore to answer. 'As I was saying, in all my years of teaching, I have never, and I mean never, had a student as disruptive and disinclined to work as your daughter. It's also possible I've never had one as bright. *That's* why I keep on trying to challenge her—to get her to use her brain. It's my job to try, you know. And as her father, you might understand that.'

The man so close to her on the opposite stool moved his legs, so that once again they almost touched hers. She inched away, and looked doubtfully at his face, wondering what on earth had got into her to speak to him like that.

Heavy lids shielded his eyes and she couldn't tell what he was thinking when he replied quietly, 'If what you say is true, Miss Reid, why is it that Tasmin is doing quite well in all her other classes?'

Rosemary stared at him reflectively. His handsome head was bent slightly forward now and he appeared to be studying the brown leather brogues stretched casually in front of him. For a moment she didn't reply to his question, and when she did her answer came slowly, in carefully considered phrases.

'I don't think you can say she does "quite well" in her other classes. She's a little above average, I understand, but so are a great many others. Tamsin is capable of much more.'

The man in front of her lifted his head quickly, and Rosemary was subjected to the full force of his impatient grey gaze.

'That doesn't answer my question, Miss Reid.'

'No.' Rosemary pleated a fold in her slightly stained lab coat, then shoved her hand hastily into the pocket when she saw him watching her fingers. Not that she was really nervous, she told herself, she was just trying to marshal her thoughts. But there was something about Tamsin's father which made it difficult to concentrate. She tried again.

'No. You're right. That's not the whole answer. For one thing, Tamsin isn't particularly interested in biology, and perhaps she makes more of an effort in the subjects she cares about.'

'She doesn't care about maths, Miss Reid, but she does all right in it.' Now he sounded bored.

'Yes, I know,' agreed Rosemary quickly, remembering Henry Parkinson's comment about Tamsin's terminal allergy to work. 'But "all right" is not the same as doing well. And really, by the age of sixteen the students have to start taking some responsibility for themselves. Tamsin doesn't seem to have discovered that yet.'

'Really.' A muscle moved at the corner of his eye, but the seductive voice was very smooth. 'And yet, according to my daughter, you continue to push her unmercifully. Is that letting her take responsibility for herself?'

Rosemary shifted uncomfortably on the stool. 'I believe it's encouraging her to do so, yes.' She raised her eyes and looked him full in the face. 'There is also the fact that I have a number of students in my class besides Tamsin. As I said before, she's very disruptive and sometimes I have to insist on her co-operation just so that the others can get on with their work. Mr Riordan, I would love to have a better relationship with your daughter. I would also love it if she would even occasionally arrive in class on time, listen to my instructions, keep quiet while I am talking, stop interfering with those who are trying to work, and——' she waved at the microscope standing beside the unwashed dissecting pan '——put her equipment away when she has finished with it. Unfortunately, those things seem to be beyond her capabilities.'

The smoke-grey eyes stared back at her, and behind their opaque inscrutability Rosemary thought she detected a quiet, almost smouldering antagonism. But it was not only antagonism, it was something even stronger—— something very physical that jolted like a current between them.

'What you say may be partially true, Miss Reid,' he was replying coldly. 'I know my daughter isn't always easy.' He passed a hand briefly across his forehead, and she noticed the minute lines spreading from the corners of his eyes. 'She lost her mother six years ago, and I'm probably not the world's greatest father. But I hardly think you're helping her by singling her out from the others, sending her out of the room almost every day on some pretext or other, constantly questioning her efforts— and making an issue of trivialities like forgetting to return a microscope.'

He straightened and rose to his feet. Rosemary stood up, too. Her head just reached his chin, and suddenly she felt a great wave of indignation sweep over her. She had had a long, frustrating day, she was very tired, and now this rude, domineering and thoroughly disconcerting man was towering over her in her own classroom, calmly informing her that the school's expensive microscopes were trivialities—presumably provided for the exclusive amusement of his spoiled and equally trying daughter.

Rosemary abandoned all efforts at control, and with her long feet extended like a dancer's put her hands on her hips and shouted at him.

'*You* may think the school's equipment doesn't matter, Mr Riordan, but I assure you that if microscopes are not put away properly with the stage down and the condenser up, when the next person tries to use them, there's a good chance the lens could be broken. And with funds as tight as they are we may not get a replacement. I suppose that doesn't matter to you, does it? Your delightful daughter can just grab another one to wreck—and to hell with everybody else.'

He was staring at her, his strong face hard and unreadable. Rosemary dropped her eyes, and saw large fists bunch together at his waist. She stepped back hastily and sank down on the stool, her fury dying out as quickly as it had flared, as she became aware that she had just conducted the worst parent-teacher interview of her life. Her handling of it had been quite unbelievably bad. How could she have lost control like that? Granted, the provocation had been considerable, and it had been a dreadful day, but that was certainly no excuse.

The big hands clenched in front of her opened slowly, and she looked up into his face. It was very still, the square jaw jutting upwards and the full-lipped mouth a straight, uncompromising line.

'Obviously you don't like my daughter, Miss Reid. Under the circumstances, I think it will be better for all concerned if she transfers out of your class. I'll speak to the principal in the morning.'

All the fight had gone out of Rosemary now, and she felt bone weary, and drained.

'Very well, Mr Riordan,' she replied tonelessly.

He threw her a brief, disgusted glance, and a spark of her old spirit returned. 'You'll have trouble seeing the principal, though. In case you've forgotten, it's Saturday tomorrow.'

She saw his nostrils flare briefly, and then his lips twisted in an odd little grimace as he spun on his heel and strode silently out of the room. She watched his long thighs move sinuously in the well-fitting beige trousers.

Damn! Rosemary pushed herself slowly off the stool, placed Tamsin's dissecting pan in the sink and trailed unhappily back to her desk. But she couldn't seem to concentrate on marking now, and in any case Mrs Fong was due any minute. Another parent. She sighed, feeling limp and suddenly unable to cope.

What on earth had gone wrong with that interview? She had dealt with irate parents before, but had never come so close to losing her temper as she had done today. If Mr Riordan reported it to the principal, she was in for a very uncomfortable session on Monday. And, what was more, it would be entirely her own fault. He had every right to

complain—even if he was rude, smug and impossible and
had brought most of it on himself. Yes, he *was* a perfect
beast of a man. Perhaps that was the trouble. Beast he
might be, but his body was almost too perfect . . .

Stop it, Rosemary, she told herself firmly. You moved
to Vancouver to get away from exactly that sort of thing.
You fell for Ronald because of his looks, and see where
that got you.

In fact it had got her to Vancouver. But the purpose of
the move, she reminded herself firmly, had *not* been to go
suddenly moonstruck because some arrogant male with a
difficult daughter also happened to have a nice back view
in a pair of trousers.

Exasperating, ill-mannered beast, she muttered to
herself.

And it wasn't true what he said. She didn't dislike
Tamsin. Just the opposite, really. Although the girl made
life awkward for her at times, there was something very
appealing about the clever, disruptive teenager.

She shrugged. It didn't matter now, anyhow. Tamsin's
father was having her transferred out of the class.

A polite coughing sound came from the outer lab, and
Rosemary put down her pen. She would finish the
marking over the weekend. Right now she must deal with
Mrs Fong.

Rosemary hurried down the grey, stone steps of the school
and made her way towards the car park.

The interview with Mrs Fong had gone predictably well,
in spite of the fact that she had had to keep a tight rein on
her responses to the pleasant little woman's questions
—mainly because Mr Riordan has aroused in her a
resentful, and quite unfair, suspicion of all parents

today. But she knew the feeling wouldn't last.

Her head was bent against the fine March rain which had been drizzling down since early morning, and she was so absorbed in her thoughts that she didn't see the bulky figure standing beside the green late-model Lincoln in the sloping car park until she had almost run him down.

'What the hell . . .' exclaimed an uncomfortably familiar voice from somewhere above her head. There was silence for a moment as the owner of the voice took Rosemary gently by the shoulders and held her away from him. 'Ah, I see,' he continued, as grey eyes examined her startled face against the damp, cloud-swept background. 'The indomitable Miss Reid, en route to a wild weekend with the schoolbooks, I suppose.'

He gestured at the bundle of marking she had balanced beneath her arm.

Rosemary shifted the papers uneasily against her waist, and dropped the whole unwieldy package in a puddle.

# CHAPTER TWO

'NICE going,' remarked Rosemary's nemesis, in a voice which still seemed to come from on high, because she had sunk quickly to her knees and was scrabbling frantically in the puddle to rescue her students' work before it disintegrated.

'Oh dear,' she groaned, oblivious now of the man still towering above her. She pulled a dripping wad of papers from a watery grave and tried to tuck it under her heavy, fawn-coloured duffel-coat.

'You'll have much more luck if you unzip it first,' observed the voice which had caused her to drop the papers in the first place. 'Here, let me help.'

Before Rosemary had time to stop him, he had bent down, unfastened her coat and removed the sopping homework from her fingers. The next moment it had been pressed quickly against her chest and his hand was at the base of her throat as he pulled the zipper securely up to her neck.

She swallowed, and for the first time lifted her eyes. For a brief moment they locked with his. Then she tore them quickly away and saw that the figure crouched so close to her that their knees were touching was no longer wearing a jacket. In fact, to Rosemary's startled gaze, for a moment he appeared to be wearing nothing above the waist. Then she realised that the pale, peach-coloured shirt was plastered so closely to his body that it gave the illusion of skin. Beneath the wet fabric she could see corded muscles tensed against the cold as he took her hands and pulled her to her feet.

'You're very quiet all of a sudden, Miss Reid.' He gave her a rather bleak smile and added softly, 'And if you don't get that very wet schoolwork to safety as soon as possible, you're likely to catch pneumonia.'

'No, I'm not,' said Rosemary, assuming her teacher role automatically. 'You catch colds from viruses, not from getting wet.'

'I was merely expressing concern,' he replied tersely, 'not fishing for a lecture on microbiology.'

'Oh. Thank you.' She started to turn away, then hesitated. 'Why?'

'Why what?'

'Why should you be concerned? My welfare didn't seem to be much of a priority when we met half an hour ago.'

'Didn't it? Well, I still think you should get that bundle of soggy verbiage away from your chest, Miss Reid. I doubt if anyone's homework is worth dying for. Particularly not my daughter's, so you tell me.'

'I've no intention of dying,' she replied tartly. 'And what makes you think I'm carrying Tamsin's homework here?' She tapped the bulge in the front of her coat and glared challengingly at the complacent, very damp man leaning so casually against the Lincoln.

'It's on top. I'm familiar with the lady's handwriting, believe it or not.'

'So am I,' muttered Rosemary grimly, thinking of Tamsin's usual undecipherable scrawl. She drew a long, controlled breath. 'Thank you, Mr Riordan. I'll take your advice and put this stuff away.'

He nodded without replying, and she walked quickly

away from him towards her car. A minute later she had removed the saturated bundle from her coat and was slumped limply behind the wheel of her newly repaired Toyota.

She strummed her fingers thoughtfully against the dashboard. Really, the man was an enigma. In the classroom he had behaved like a typical over-indulgent father who thought the whole world ought to revolve around his daughter. Yet outside, in the damp and chill of the car park, he had taken the time to help her, and had seemed genuinely concerned that she shouldn't catch cold.

Rosemary shook her head, and turned to look over her shoulder.

He was standing with his back to her, legs slightly apart as he bent over the boot of his car. For the second time that day, she was impressed by his appearance from the rear. Then she frowned, annoyed with herself, as he slammed down the cover and began to wipe his hands on a stained white rag.

Up until now Rosemary had been so absorbed in her own problems that it had not occurred to her to wonder why he was still in the car park—without his jacket in the pouring rain. Now it came to her that he must be having trouble with his car. Serves him right, she thought grumpily. Then she sighed. Maybe it did serve him right, but it was hardly charitable of her to leave him stranded here in the rapidly approaching twilight. It wouldn't hurt her to offer him a lift to a garage.

She sighed again, and scrambled out of the Toyota.

His hands paused as Rosemary approached him, and he threw the rag carelessly into the car.

'Back again, Miss Reid?' he asked lightly, pulling

out his jacket and slinging it over his shoulders.

Rosemary nodded, her eyes travelling unwillingly to the sinuous strength of his forearms as he buttoned the sleeves of his shirt. 'I thought you might need a lift,' she explained briskly. 'I see you're having trouble.'

'Not any more,' he replied. 'I've just finished changing a tyre.'

Rosemary looked at his legs and for the first time it registered that his well-tailored trousers were covered in gravel. Of course. That explained the absence of a jacket—and the skin-tight, peach-coloured shirt.

'Oh, I see.' She smiled awkwardly, feeling suddenly embarrassed. She certainly didn't want this man to think she was making too-friendly overtures.

'It's good of you to offer, though,' he was saying, 'especially after the less than amiable discussion we had earlier.' He smiled back at her, a slow, reserved smile, and for a moment Rosemary had the impression he was as uncomfortable as she was. Then he spoiled it by adding, 'But it won't change my mind about Tamsin, you know.'

'I didn't imagine it would,' she said quickly. 'And it wasn't particularly good of me. I live in Richmond anyway, so almost everything is on my way.'

'Is it? I wouldn't have thought so.' He closed his eyes as the wind blasted a gust of rain against his face. 'My partner's Aunt Alice lives in Richmond,' he remarked non-committally.

Rosemary's eyes widened in surprise. Was he actually making an effort to be pleasant?

'Are you making conversation?' she asked disbelievingly.

He gave a small smile. 'Hardly. No one in his right

mind would choose to make conversation in the middle of a school car park, in a saturated shirt, on one of the wettest, most miserable evenings Vancouver has experienced so far this year. And I haven't lost my mind yet, Miss Reid.'

'Oh. Well, I didn't think you had.' She was about to bid him a hasty farewell, when the import of his earlier words sunk in.

'Did you say Aunt *Alice*?' she asked, pausing in the act of spinning around to hurry back to her car. 'You don't mean Alice Maloney, by any chance?'

His eyelids, which had been half closed against the weather, arched up quickly to reveal the startled depths of his arresting eyes.

'How did you know that?' He paused, and Rosemary saw surprise replaced by comprehension. 'Oh, I see. I suppose she lives somewhere near you.'

Rosemary smiled smugly. 'Yes. As a matter of fact, Alice Maloney and her duck-tolling retrievers are my next-door neighbours.'

He lifted his head quickly, and she saw the raindrops glistening on his hair and the amused astonishment in his eyes. 'I don't believe it,' he exclaimed. 'Tamsin's terrible teacher turns out to be Scheming Alice's "charming child next door".'

Rosemary shifted her bag on her shoulder and glared at him. 'There's no need to be rude about Alice,' she said frigidly. 'She's been very kind to me. And I'm hardly a charming child.'

'You can say that again,' agreed Tamsin's father, with much more fervour than was flattering.

'Thank you,' she replied sourly. 'Mine is not the only personality around here that leaves something to be

desired.' This time she did not pause as she turned away
from him, and her fingers were already on the handle of
her car before she realised that a heavy, masculine hand
was gripping her shoulder.

'Now what is it?' she asked irritably, not bothering to
turn around.

His hand tightened on her shoulder. 'You didn't say
goodnight,' he murmured softly. Rosemary heard the
mocking note in his voice, and almost stamped her foot.

'Good*night*,' she muttered, with far more emphasis
than she intended.

Her shoulder was released abruptly, and she felt an odd
little pang of regret. More irritable than ever, she pulled
open the door of the Toyota and thumped herself down
behind the wheel.

The cause of her bad temper, with a small shrug, strode
back across the car park and slid quickly into the Lincoln.

A minute later the car park was empty as two cars
driven by tight-lipped, glowering owners encountered each
other at the exit and drove off in opposite directions.


Jonathan Riordan pushed back the sheet which was
covering his face and slowly opened his eyes. Outside the
window of the white-painted, Point Gray home which his
partner called 'venerably mellow', the blossoms on the
wild plum tree beside the garden wall were just beginning
to bud. Jonathan stared at the gently waving branches
with their tantalising promise of spring, and wondered
why he was in a bad mood before the day had even started.

Then one pink twig whipped rapidly against the wall
and snapped—and he remembered.

Tamsin. Miss Reid. That frustrating interview of the
day before. He flung the covers off, eased himself out of

bed and reached for his jeans and sweater.

Downstairs in the kitchen, Tamsin was clumping about making coffee and complaining because there were no eggs.

'Aren't there?' said Jonathan without much interest. 'I expect Mrs Peacock forgot them.'

'She's always forgetting,' grumbled Tamsin crossly, thumping her sturdy young body down noisily in the nearest chair. 'Mother never forgot.'

Jonathan closed his eyes. 'No, I suppose she didn't. But that was a long time ago, Tamsin. We don't manage too badly without her, do we?'

Tamsin frowned and tipped three spoonfuls of sugar into her cup. 'No, I guess not—but—you know what, Dad? I think you ought to get married again.'

She stirred the sugar vigorously and fixed large brown eyes meditatively on her father's face.

Jonathan choked into his coffee. 'I ought to *what*?'

'Get married again.'

'Good God.' He put his cup down hastily on the table, pulled out a chair and sat down heavily across from Tamsin. 'Are you trying to tell me I should get married again because we're out of eggs?'

Tamsin giggled. 'No, of course not. But—oh, I don't know. This house seems lonely sometimes with just the two of us here. And lately you've seemed lonely too and—well——'

'Bad-tempered,' finished Jonathan drily. 'I know, and I'm sorry. That's because I've had some problems with the business. Not serious ones, though, and they're well under control. As for being lonely—I don't exactly lack female companionship—if I want it.'

'Yeah, I'd noticed. Bunch of gold-diggers,' muttered

Tamsin.

Jonathan stood up and poured himself another cup of coffee. With his back to Tamsin, she couldn't see his lips twitch up at the corners. 'What did you say?' he asked ominously, still with his face averted.

Tamsin swallowed. 'I just meant that since you run a mining exploration company—I mean, gold is part of mining . . .' Her voice trailed off uncertainly, and Jonathan spun around.

There was a faintly malicious glint in his grey eyes now as he murmured thoughtfully, 'Well, of course, if you don't like my usual choice of ladies, I could always approach that charming teacher of yours . . .'

'Miss Reid?' Tamsin's voice rose in a squeak. 'Dad, are you having me on?'

Jonathan eyed her blandly over the top of his cup. 'Why should I do that?'

'Because you always do.'

'Do I? Well, the fact is I met the fair Miss Reid yesterday.' He put his cup down and leaned towards her, his eyes serious now, and a little hard. 'She said you have a very good brain—which you aren't using—and that you're a damned disruptive nuisance in her class.'

'She *didn't* say that?' gasped Tamsin indignantly.

'Not in so many words—but that's what she meant.'

'Oh.' Tamsin digested this. 'What did *you* say?'

Jonathan smiled austerely. 'I said a great many things I shouldn't have, and eventually told her you would be transferring out of her class.'

'*Dad*, what did you do that for?' wailed Tamsin.

Jonathan wondered the same thing. He thought of the willowy, fair-haired girl with the heart-shaped face and freckles, and the long ballet-dancer's feet, who had stood flashing her golden eyes at him across that hopelessly cluttered lab. Why *had* he got off on that drastically wrong foot with her? Somehow she had got under his skin . . .

'I'm not at all sure,' he said finally, in answer to Tamsin's question. 'In any case, I imagine you'll be pleased.'

'But I don't want to transfer. The other biology class is full. And anyway, I don't like Mr Chen.'

'You don't like Miss Reid, either.'

'She's not all that bad,' Tamsin muttered grudgingly.

'In other words, I was out there on a wild-goose chase yesterday. And Miss Reid was absolutely right about your behaviour.' Jonathan's voice was stern now, and Tamsin glanced uneasily at his large hands resting on the table. He had always been easy-going, but she knew all too well that there was a point beyond which it was unwise to push her father.

'I guess she *was* right,' admitted Tamsin in a very small voice. 'Do I have to transfer out of her class?'

Jonathan eyed his daughter grimly. 'No. In fact, I'll do my best to see you stay there. I can't think of anyone better equipped to cope with your nonsense than that remarkably self-confident young woman.'

Tamsin, deciding discretion was the better part of valour, nodded hastily and scuttled out of the room.

Jonathan sighed and stared thoughtfully at the plum tree spreading its branches at the bright spring sun which had promisingly followed the rain. He began to strum his fingers on the table.

Then he reached his arm for the telephone on the counter, and slowly spun the dial.

'Hi.' The familiar voice of his partner bounced cheerfully over the wires. 'How's it going, Johnno?'

'Fine. Derek?'

'Mm-hm? I know that tone of voice. You want something. Right?'

Jonathan cleared his throat. 'Right. How do you feel about hospitals, old friend?'

There was a choking sound on the other end of the line. 'Not great. When I was in to have that cyst removed, I was guarded night and day by a succession of fire-breathing dragons in white who kept trying to feed me jelly. I ask you. Jelly.' His voice dropped to a disgusted croak. 'Why? What about hospitals?'

Jonathan laughed, but there was a slight note of strain in his voice when he replied. 'As a matter of fact,' he said carefully, 'I was wondering if you could manage to have your appendix out—just temporarily, of course.'

Cheese, thought Rosemary, as she skidded her cart round the supermarket. And eggs . . .

Unexpectedly, and rather irritatingly, the image of Tamsin's obnoxious father popped suddenly into her head. To her considerable annoyance this had happened several times since that abortive meeting yesterday. But in spite of her resentment she couldn't help wondering if he and Tamsin lived on cheese and eggs, as she so often did. No, of course they didn't. That tiresomely capable hunk with his aura of quiet affluence probably had a housekeeper to do his cooking. A pretty, long-legged one, no doubt—with big breasts.

'I beg your pardon!'

Rosemary started and, raising her eyes from a display of canned sardines, found herself looking into the indignantly gaping face of a well-endowed matron in pink. Oh, dear. She must have been muttering out loud.

'Oh. Sorry. Didn't mean you . . .' she mumbled idiotically.

When the woman's chest swelled visibly to even more impressive proportions, Rosemary decided she was only making things worse. With another quick apology she removed herself hastily to the next aisle.

And it's all that beastly man's fault, she told herself furiously and with a complete disregard for fairness. She picked up a packet of Minute Rice and glanced quickly at her watch.

Help! It was after five. And she had to be at Alice's by seven. She gave the contents of her cart a cursory checkover and hurried to the cashier's stand.

Three-quarters of an hour later the Toyota bumped its way over a collection of pot-holes and pulled into her driveway. Not for the first time, she wondered if she had made the right decision when she had elected to rent a two-bedroom bungalow in suburban Richmond, instead of settling for something conveniently close to the school. She had made her choice because out here she could enjoy the illusion of being in the country, living on the flat, drained delta farmland, with Alice and her dogs next door. But the pot-holes were really getting beyond a joke. And so was Alice, with her royal command to attend this Dog Club Banquet tonight.

Speak of the devil! As Rosemary heaved groceries out of her car, a small ginger-coloured dog trotted past her and stuck his nose hopefully into a bag of cheese and biscuits.

'Get out of there, Murphy,' shouted the cause of Rosemary's irritation. The white-haired old lady was standing on the front porch next door, supervising Rosemary's arrival. Murphy reluctantly removed his nose, and Alice added in a strong commanding voice, 'Don't be late, Rosemary. Seven o'clock, remember.'

'Yes. I'll be there, Alice.'

Frowning slightly, she carried the remainder of her groceries inside and started to put them away.

Alice and her dogs, she groaned to herself as a jar of pickles fell over in the fridge. Who but Alice Maloney would think of breeding dogs with the unlikely name of Nova Scotia duck-tolling retrievers? And, if it wasn't for Alice, she wouldn't be going to this doggy banquet tonight and could have attended the classical guitar concert with Ann and Len from school. But old Alice was amazingly persistent and persuasive. And as usual she had got her own way.

Rosemary frowned again. She really was *not* anxious to spend the evening listening to a lot of doggy dowagers discussing doggy diets, and the unfairness of judges in general and the one in particular who had just rejected their precious Bingo or Snoopy in favour of an animated dishmop for Best in Show.

She had been to a dog show once, and was not anxious to repeat the experience.

Still, there was no help for it. To the banquet she must go. She sighed, and retrieved a can of baked beans from the floor. Scheming Alice, that horrible man had called her. She pressed her lips together disapprovingly, but found they wouldn't stay that way and started to grin instead.

The description was all too apt.

Rosemary had agreed to pick up her elderly neighbour from next door, because Alice had complained that her car was not running properly and she needed a ride to the banquet. Funny, that. She wasn't surprised that Alice was having car problems. The old lady drove her battered station wagon like a tank. What did puzzle Rosemary a bit was that her very bright and totally unsenile neighbour had apparently left the problem unattended to.

She was even more puzzled when she pulled the Toyota into the weed-covered driveway of the white stucco bungalow next door, to find it was occupied not only by the station wagon but by a dark green Lincoln which looked oddly familiar.

Rosemary climbed out of her car and stared at the interloper. For some reason her mind was unwilling to make the obvious connection, and it was not until Alice opened the door and two ecstatic tollers hurled themselves towards her that she lifted her eyes, saw the tall man standing behind Alice and realised she had been well and truly had.

# CHAPTER THREE

'AH, there you are, my dear,' beamed Alice, her small, erect figure tripping down the steps to greet her guest. 'You look quite charming in that soft green silk.'

Rosemary was well aware that the draped folds of the silk accentuated her slender figure, just as its colour brought out the golden highlights of her eyes. But she had worn it to make herself feel better about spending an evening going to the dogs—not to arouse that obvious gleam of approval in the eyes of the man in the beautifully tailored grey suit who had strolled down the steps behind Alice and was looking her up and down with a small, provocative smile on his sensuously curving lips. Rosemary felt her heart thump as a familiar flash of excitement stirred somewhere below her waist. She frowned quickly, astounded at the confused thoughts that were running through her mind, and trying desperately to control the unwanted sensations that were cascading through her body.

The smiling old lady with her cloud of beautiful white hair was watching her with bright, beady eyes. 'Rosemary, you've met Jonathan Riordan before, I understand.' The bird-like eyes turned quickly from one to the other as Rosemary and Jonathan appraised each other silently.

Rosemary's eyes dropped first. 'Yes,' she replied. 'I *used* to teach Mr Riordan's daughter.' She laid special emphasis on the word *used*, and was pleased to see him wince as he brushed a hand fleetingly across his mouth.

Score one for me, thought Rosemary. And his name is Jonathan, is it? Suits him, too. An epic sort of name—for a man who seems larger than life.

His mind must have been running along the same lines, for at that moment he stepped around Alice, held out his hand, and remarked pleasantly, 'So your name is Rosemary. That doesn't sound nearly so prim and proper as Miss Reid.' There was laughter in his grey eyes now, but Rosemary was in no mood for banter and refused to take the proffered hand. She was certain that her friend Alice had deliberately arranged this little scene—although Alice did not look as smugly triumphant as she usually did when she got her own way.

'Yes, my name is Rosemary,' she replied coldly. 'Miss Reid to you, Mr Riordan.'

'Now, my dear . . .' began Alice worriedly.

But Jonathan Riordan was laughing quite openly now. Rosemary watched the muscles strain across his chest as he raised his head and let out a shout of mirth.

'I stand corrected. Miss Reid, it is. Prim and proper as ever.'

He saw the flash of annoyance cross her face, and was suddenly contrite. 'I'm sorry,' he said quickly, the laughter leaving his eyes. 'I've ruffled your feathers again, haven't I? I don't mean to, you know.'

She read what looked like genuine contrition in his face, and wondered what in fact he *had* meant. Something inside her melted suddenly. Perhaps it was just that she had been hurrying to be on time, but somehow she didn't have the energy to fight him any more.

'Apology accepted,' she said lightly. 'Do I gather you're attending this occasion too, Mr Riordan?'

'Jonathan.'

She thought about that. 'All right. Jonathan. And *are* you coming with us?'

'If you young people don't stop sniffing round each other like a couple of dogs on heat, nobody's going to get anywhere,' Alice interrupted grumpily.

Rosemary glanced at her in surprise. Obviously things were not going quite as Alice had planned, for, although she always spoke her mind, this was the first time Rosemary had heard her speak quite so pointedly. Not looking at Jonathan, she grinned sheepishly at her neighbour and remarked that she had never been called a dog on heat before.

'Bitch would be more appropriate,' she heard Jonathan mutter as he slid behind the wheel of the Lincoln a minute later.

But she was in the back seat, and he was already pulling out of the driveway, so it hardly seemed safe to hit him.

The dog-club gathering was being held in one of the reception rooms of a large Vancouver hotel. Jonathan parked his car conveniently close to the elevator leading up from the underground parking, and made a great production of helping Alice through the sliding doors and along the carpeted hallway to the banquet-room. He took no notice of Rosemary, and she wondered if his neglect of her was deliberate provocation or just well-mannered concern for the old lady's welfare.

She pressed her lips firmly together and decided that in any case she was *not* going to be provoked. When Jonathan finally stopped fussing over Alice and came to help Rosemary with her gold angora wrap, she flashed him a bored, blatantly insincere smile, and turned to examine her hair in the mirror which was hanging beside the entrance.

'There are two out of place behind your left ear—and a grey one right here.' Firm, masculine fingers brushed the back of her neck and she felt his warm breath blow softly across her temples. But for once his closeness had very little effect on her.

'What?' she yelped. 'I couldn't have—I've never had a grey hair in my life.'

She whirled round to face him, the long hair under discussion swinging freely about her shoulders—and saw that his maddeningly attractive mouth was parted in a grin of pure devilment.

'Oh!' she cried. 'You beast. You said that on purpose to scare the pants off me, didn't you?'

The grin broadened. 'Well, that's a charming thought,' he began.

Rosemary felt an almost irresistible urge to kick him, and only the realisation that Alice was watching them with a small, slightly pained smile on her lips caused her to interrupt frostily, 'That is *not* what I meant, Mr Riordan, and you know it. Now, don't you think it's time you returned your attentions to Alice? She's waiting for us to see her to her table.'

He was still grinning as he complied with her suggestion and turned obligingly to Alice.

'We're at the head table because I'm on the executive,' the old lady informed Jonathan as he escorted her down the length of the room. She cocked her head at him knowingly. 'And I hope you two manage to behave yourselves this evening. This was not what I had in mind, you know.'

'I always behave myself,' replied Jonathan, his grey eyes

widening innocently. 'What *did* you have in mind, Aunt Alice?'

'I'm not your Aunt Alice, and you know very well what I had in mind,' replied Alice tartly. But her words were softened by a brief, resigned smile.

Rosemary found herself seated between Jonathan and a slightly deaf old gentleman who was carrying on a loud, one-sided conversation about ears with the woman on his left.

'I think he means dogs' ears,' whispered Jonathan, observing her startled expression. 'And you don't have a grey hair on your lovely head, Miss Reid. As for scaring the pants off you . . .'

'You wouldn't stand a chance,' she interrupted tartly.

But his fair head was bent very close to hers and his eyes were so bland and deliberately guileless that Rosemary suddenly felt her ill humour evaporate. The amusement he was pretending to hide was contagious, and his presence was intoxicatingly attractive.

'I guess I did react like an ageing prima donna, didn't I?' She smiled ruefully. 'And I might as well get used to the idea. Grey hair will come soon enough, I suppose, and I can't have a fit of the vapours every time a new one comes to light.'

'As far as I'm concerned you can,' retorted Jonathan. 'I thoroughly enjoyed your vapours.'

'Yes, so I noticed,' replied Rosemary drily. 'But . . .' She paused, because she saw he was not listening to her. Instead his eyes were fixed gloomily on the array of cutlery laid out on the clean white cloth.

'What's the matter?' she asked, puzzled.

'Nothing terminal. It's just that I'm beginning to see evidence that a vast quantity is about to be served to this canine congregation. And before I left home I was obliged to consume three pieces of a disastrous carrot cake which my thoroughly undomesticated daughter suddenly took it into her head to produce for my delectation. I hadn't the heart to refuse her.'

'Commendably paternal of you,' remarked Rosemary smugly.

'And there's no need to gloat,' he replied severely.

She looked at him curiously, her light brown eyes appearing more golden than ever in the dim lighting of the banquet-hall.

'But you must have known you'd have to eat,' she objected. 'Although I'm not sure I understand what you're doing here. I mean—well, when I saw that cagey look on Alice's face as she opened the door this evening, I knew she was plotting something—and I supposed the something must be you.'

He curved a large hand thoughtfully round the stem of his wineglass, and he was not looking at her when he replied levelly, 'No, actually it was my partner, Derek.'

Rosemary blinked. 'Your partner—I don't understand.'

His mouth twisted wryly. 'Alice Maloney is devoted to her nephew Derek. Aren't you, Alice?' He turned to his partner on the right, but Alice was absorbed in an animated conversation about the iniquities of the American Kennel Club with the military-looking man on her other side, and she appeared not to have heard him. He turned back to Rosemary.

'Alice brought Derek up, you see,' he explained. 'And she doesn't altogether approve of his having reached the ripe old age of thirty-six without having settled down with a nice, preferably dog-loving wife, to raise a new generation of Dereks.'

Rosemary laughed. 'But she's never settled down herself,' she protested. 'Or, at least, I doubt if she had ever done a single thing she doesn't want to do.'

Jonathan placed his arm casually along the back of her chair, and she felt a disconcerting quiver of excitement. 'You're probably right. But Derek says she thinks men need a steadying influence. And Bozo's not it.'

'Bozo?' Rosemary echoed faintly.

'Mm. Derek's current ladyfriend.'

'With a name like that, Alice may have a point,' murmured Rosemary. 'But I still don't see what that has to do with your being here.'

'Ah.' Jonathan shifted his arm so that it dropped loosely over her shoulder. 'Well, you see . . .' He was staring across the room at a picture on the opposite wall, and Rosemary could not read his eyes. 'You see, Bozo is in Zimbabwe at the moment—she's always off some-where—so Derek said all right, he'd go to this dog dance and meet Alice's charming child next door. He figured he might as well please his favourite aunt . . .' He withdrew his eyes from the wall and glanced quickly at Alice, but she was still holding forth about the American Kennel Club. 'In fact, though, I knew he didn't like the idea—what he really likes is Bozo—and after I met you yesterday and made some rather uncalled-for remarks about your teaching methods . . .'

'They were more than uncalled-for, Mr Riordan. They were rude and insulting.'

He lifted an eyebrow. 'That bad? And am I Mr Riordan again? Would an apology make a difference?'

'Whose?' asked Rosemary suspiciously.

'Mine, of course. I knew I'd made a mistake when I told Tamsin that she was transferring from your class and she dug all ten toes in and asked if she could stay.' He smiled ruefully. 'I love my daughter, but there are times when I could cheerfully wring her neck.'

'Yes,' agreed Rosemary. 'With a classful of thirty adolescents, I'm familiar with the feeling. Apology accepted.'

'Good.' He ran his thumb lightly down her cheek, and the look in his smoky eyes was suddenly so seductive that Rosemary would have accepted an apology for mayhem.

Fortunately, at that moment the soup arrived, and it was several minutes before Rosemary was able to return to the subject of his presence at the banquet.

'What *are* you doing at this doggy celebration?' she asked curiously, as a waiter cleared the bowls.

'Mm? Oh, I see. Well, for one thing, as I said, I felt I owed you an apology—so I persuaded Derek to succumb to an attack of appendicitis.'

Rosemary took a deep breath. 'And what,' she said, in an ominously quiet voice, 'do you think you're talking about, Mr—Jonathan?'

Jonathan stared glumly at a large plate of roast beef and potatoes which the waiter had placed in front of him. 'Actually, we decided on indigestion in the end. Appendicitis seemed overdoing it a bit.'

'Mr—Jonathan . . .' began Rosemary threateningly.

He held up his hand. 'All right, don't stab me with that menacing cutlery you're wielding . . .'

Rosemary glanced at her hand and put her bread knife down hastily.

'That's better. Now, as I was about to explain, I persuaded Derek to let me take his place. As he wasn't keen to come in the first place, he didn't take much persuading.'

'Very flattering,' murmured Rosemary. She pushed a forkful of mixed vegetables thoughtfully around her plate. 'You said for one thing you thought you owed me an apology. Is there some other reason why you're here?'

'Yes, very definitely. I wanted to let you know that Tamsin won't be leaving your class, after all.'

'You could have phoned the school about that, you know. And what makes you think I'm anxious to keep Tamsin, Mr—Jonathan?' For some reason she felt obscurely cheated that Jonathan's main reason for attending this occasion appeared to be the rearrangement of his daughter's timetable.

'But I didn't want to phone,' he was saying calmly. 'I wanted to see you again. And I didn't in the least imagine you were anxious to keep Tamsin. That's why I decided to talk to you. Oh—and one more thing.' His fingers brushed against her hair. 'My name is not Mr Jonathan.'

Rosemary looked up at him and her breath caught awkwardly in her throat. She saw the gleam of amusement in his eyes as he added softly, 'It's Jonathan to you, Rosemary.' His voice was almost a caress. 'Not Mr Riordan, not Mr Jonathan, just Jonathan.'

She was hypnotised by his eyes. They were fixed on her with a mocking, seductive warmth, and for a moment she felt she would drown in their languorous grey depths. Then she gave herself an abrupt mental shake, turned her head away and chirped brightly, 'All right. Jonathan, then. Aren't you going to eat this delicious roast beef?'

The warmth faded from his eyes and, although the amusement was still there, the look he gave her now was one of disgruntled reproach.

'Do you ask merely for information?' he enquired. 'Or was that remark made with deliberate malice?'

Rosemary grinned. 'Mostly malice, I think,' she replied cheerfully. 'Aren't you enjoying it, Jonathan?'

He caught the hesitation in her voice as she pronounced his name, and smiled, a little grimly. 'I am making a supreme effort to be polite,' he informed her, 'but the carrot cake was a mistake.' He placed a piece of meat between his teeth. Once more he held her with his eyes as he bit into it, slowly. Rosemary felt something warm and sensual curl up inside her . . .

This was getting ridiculous. Alice's dog-club banquet which she had expected to endure with bored equanimity was turning into an exercise in foreplay the like of which she had never experienced before. And it had to stop. Now.

'I'm glad Tamsin will be staying in my class,' she said quickly, switching the subject to safely prosaic channels.

'Are you? Then my estimation of your character was correct.'

Rosemary looked at him suspiciously. 'What estimation?' she asked, not feeling at all certain she wanted to hear the answer.

He grinned. 'That you have stamina, tolerance, endurance, dedication—and the obstinate tenacity of a dog with a difficult bone.'

Rosemary laughed, not sure whether to take his words as compliment or insult. 'Are you referring to your daughter as a bone?' she asked lightly.

He thought about it, then sighed and said resignedly, 'That's one of my more charitable descriptions of the lady.'

Rosemary decided this was neither the time nor the place for a discussion of Jonathan's relationship with his daughter. 'In that case, I think this gourmet débâcle serves you right,' she remarked primly.

'Oh, hardly a débâcle.' The gleam in his eye was back. 'After all, I wanted to talk to you. And I am.' He smiled complacently.

His arm was across the back of her chair again and he was caressing her with his eyes. Rosemary switched her attention quickly to the man on her left.

Half an hour later, white-coated figures began to clear the tables and a lanky young man with a moustache appeared, to fidget busily with the controls of a collection of electronic boxes. The dim lights were turned even lower.

'I want to talk to you, young man.' Alice turned abruptly away from her military friend, and gave Jonathan an accusing stare. 'You and my nephew have been up to something.' The determined old eyes were fixed on his in demanding expectation, and Jonathan, with a disarming smile, rose to his feet and asked if she would care to dance.

'Don't you try to bamboozle me with your blarney,' snorted Alice. But she sprang to her feet with alacrity as the man with the electronic paraphernalia pushed a button, and the strains of 'Some Enchanted Evening' began to waft softly across the room.

'Now, young man,' said Alice firmly, as Jonathan guided her expertly across the floor, '*what* is all this about?'

'About?' queried Jonathan, raising his eyebrows in assumed bewilderment.

'You know what I mean. Why has my nephew, who has never allowed anything to come between him and a pretty girl, suddenly taken to his bed with nothing more pressing than an attack of indigestion? It's not like him. And it's not like him to let me down either. What have you done to him?'

Jonathan looked down at the bristling old lady in his arms and replied with quiet sincerity, 'Nothing, I promise you. And you're right. Derek's not ill. You see . . .' He paused, remembering he was not dealing with a client whose mineral deposits had turned out to be an illusion, but with an indignant elderly aunt who wanted the best of all possible worlds for her nephew. 'You see, Derek really is fond of Bozo, so I knew he wouldn't mind my taking his place tonight—and I very much wanted to see Rosemary again. I was quite unpardonably rude to her when we first met yesterday—and I needed to talk to her.'

'Indeed,' replied the old lady sourly. 'There are telephones, you know, Mr Riordan.'

'I do know,' he confessed, whirling her round a corner with unnecessary speed, 'but quite frankly, I thought she might hang up on me.'

'Huh,' snorted Alice. 'From what I've seen tonight, I doubt it. Just like two of my tollers . . .'

'Yes, so you said,' he interrupted hastily. 'Miss Maloney, I sincerely apologise if I have spoiled your plans for Derek—but I promise you there was never much chance of his hitting it off with Rosemary. For one thing he's in love with Bozo, and for another, with a face and figure like Miss Reid's, I've no doubt she is also otherwise engaged.'

'I know her rather better than you do, young man, and I can assure you that her otherwise engagement is over. And as for Derek—I'm well aware that he is in love with—*Bozo*.' She shuddered slightly. 'But that's no reason to give up on him in despair. Quite the contrary.' She glared at Jonathan and then, slowly, the severe, disapproving look faded and she smiled, shaking her head resignedly.

'All right, Mr Riordan,' she sighed, the lines of her face blurring softly as a faraway look came into her eyes. 'I remember what it was like to be young, whatever you may think. All the same, you're a scamp—and my nephew is a damned fool.' She pushed his arm from her waist and turned away from him. 'Come along. This "enchanted evening" is not over, even if the music is—and I'm sure Rosemary is anxious to dance.'

But, when they got back to the table, Rosemary was dancing with the military gentleman. Alice headed immediately for a clutch of stout, gesticulating matrons in the far corner of the room and Jonathan sat down and reached absently for his glass.

So he was a scamp, was he? At thirty-eight years old, and with a sixteen-year-old daughter to boot, it was a long time since anyone had called him that. And Alice had said that Rosemary had been engaged once but was not any longer. Fleetingly, he wondered what it would be like to be engaged to Rosemary Reid. His lips twisted. Not dull, anyway. Not that it mattered, because entanglements of that sort were something to be avoided like the plague. A less permanent liaison, though . . . that might be—stimulating. Rosemary attracted him. And he had a feeling she was not entirely immune to him, either.

He smiled meditatively and lifted his glass to the light.

The man playing the tapes put on something loud, fast and modern, and Rosemary's military partner returned her quickly to her seat. The floor emptied rapidly as most of the middle-aged dog-fanciers decided it was time to take a break.

Jonathan swivelled slowly around to face Rosemary. 'Would you like to dance?' he asked, leaning back casually in his chair and watching her lazily from under lowered lids.

'Are you sure Alice hasn't already exhausted you?' she asked sarcastically. But there was a bantering note in her voice which belied the sharpness of her words.

'I'll show you,' he replied, taking her by the hand and pulling her to her feet with such speed that she was left gasping. A glass of white wine which she held in her hand tilted sideways and spilled its contents on the tablecloth.

'Idiot,' she muttered, dabbing a napkin at the spreading stain. 'Now look what you've done.'

'What have I done?' he asked, reaching a long arm over her shoulder. He removed the napkin and spun her round to face him. 'It will wash out quite easily, you know. Take it from an expert.'

'An expert what? Spiller of other people's wine?'

His eyes glinted, and his fingers pressed a little too hard on her wrist. 'On occasions, yes. But I meant I'm an expert on stains and washing.'

Rosemary was conscious that he was standing very close to her. 'Don't you have a housekeeper?' she asked quickly.

He put an arm around her waist and led her on to the floor. 'I have Mrs Peacock,' he replied, holding her tightly against him and resting his cheek on her hair as the music slowed again to a soft, sensuous beat. 'But she only comes in during the week—and accidents often happen at weekends.'

'I'll bet,' muttered Rosemary. But his hand was trailing slowly up her back now, his strong fingers pressing against her spine through the clinging green silk, and provoking a riot of delicious sensations that drove all thoughts of his housekeeping arrangements from her mind. This man was lethal, she realised suddenly, trying belatedly to pull away from him. She hardly knew him, her first encounter with him had been an unmitigated disaster, and yet here she was, pressed against him on the dance-floor and wishing very much that they were both somewhere else—somewhere very quiet and private.

His hold on her loosened as she struggled to pull away, and the grey eyes smiled down at her from what seemed to be a great height. But she was a tall woman herself. What was it about Jonathan that made him so overpowering?

The tempo of the music increased, and suddenly he swung her away from him, his lithe body moving in front of her with a raw, sinuous grace that made the blood pound in her veins. She watched his hips weave sensuously beneath the open jacket of his sleek grey suit, and she felt her own body begin to sway in time with his, as they circled each other rhythmically, eyes locked in a hot, hypnotic hold which was impossible to break.

Alice, watching them from a corner of the room, gave a small, audible snort and muttered to her startled companions that in her opinion Derek didn't know what he was missing.

The music stopped. Jonathan, his eyes still fixed unsmilingly on hers, held out a commanding hand. She took it, and without a word he led her out of the room, across the lobby and along the corridor which led to the open-air pool. He pushed open the sliding doors, and the cold air hit them like a blast of ice.

There were beads of moisture glistening on Jonathan's brow. He pulled out a handkerchief to wipe his forehead, his lips parting in a slow, knowing smile as he turned to look at Rosemary.

'Thank God for the cold winds of March,' he remarked enigmatically.

'Mm,' nodded Rosemary. 'It was hot in there, wasn't it?' For some reason she found herself staring at the still, shadowed waters of the half-lit pool, unwilling to look at him now that they were alone.

'Very hot,' he agreed. There was a hint of laughter in his voice—and something else which Rosemary could not quite interpret. No, that wasn't true. She knew only too well the meaning of that low, husky note with its undertone of sensuality. She understood it even better as she felt his arms reach over her shoulders from behind and pull her hard against his chest. His hands slid beneath her breasts, and she felt a great, langourous warmth creep over her, a sense of peace and security—mixed tantalisingly with the keen, quick flick of a desire that had no connection with security.

They stood quietly, staring at the pool for what seemed an eternity. Then, slowly, Jonathan placed his hands on her waist and turned her round to face him.

His hands were still on her waist as he bent his head towards her. She stared up at him in the shaded darkness as the cold wind blew persistently through her hair and lifted the folds of her thin silk dress. She shivered, although she could not feel the cold. Then Jonathan lowered his lips to hers—and the trembling of Rosemary's limbs, and the wild soaring in her heart, had nothing whatever to do with the winds of March, but only with the intoxicating presence of the man who held her in his arms, the man whom only yesterday she had hoped never to meet again.

# CHAPTER FOUR

AT FIRST Jonathan kissed her softly, his firm lips moving from her mouth to her neck and then to her mouth again, brushing lightly across her face and throat. But as Rosemary's arms crept round his shoulders, and her hands kneaded the muscles of his back through the fine cloth of his jacket, his kiss became harder, more imperative, and his tongue tasted the sweetness of her mouth with an intimate demand that stole the breath from her body. She was falling helplessly into a swirling vortex of sensations that were exhilarating and frightening and, as his hands moved from her waist to circle her back and pull her relentlessly against him, impossible to resist.

Then, somewhere in the night, a horn blared noisily. Rosemary started against Jonathan's chest, and his arms tightened around her.

But the spell was broken, and sanity returned.

'No . . .' she murmured, her hands jerking from his shoulders. 'No . . .' She pushed frantically at his chest, her nails catching at his throat as she sought to free herself.

'Hey, pussy cat, watch your claws.' Jonathan released her abruptly and raised an arm to finger the scratches on his neck. The seductive lips were twisted in a rueful grimace, now, and his grey eyes held an expression of wry surprise.

Rosemary gulped. 'I'm s-sorry,' she whispered, 'I didn't mean . . .'

'I know.' He extended his hand and touched her

51

cautiously on the cheek. 'What scared you away? I don't bite, you know. Well, only sometimes.' He gave her a wicked smile that made her stomach lurch alarmingly.

'I—no, of course you don't. It's just that . . .'

'That what?'

'The car horn. It startled me,' she said quickly—too quickly.

Jonathan eyed her sceptically. 'I see. I would have thought gouging holes in my neck with your fingernails was a bit of an over-reaction to a blaring horn, wouldn't you?' There was a biting note to his voice now, and Rosemary winced.

'I suppose so. I'm sorry . . .' She lowered her eyes and stared at the dimly seen cracks between the tiles of the floor.

Jonathan studied her drooping figure with an expression of tight-lipped exasperation. 'I gather one kiss has turned the prince into a frog instead of the other way around,' he said finally. 'That being the case, I suppose we might as well get back to the dog crowd.'

Before Rosemary could protest, or even decide if she wanted to protest, he had grabbed her roughly by the arm and was towing her through the doors and back along the corridor to the banquet-room. She stumbled behind him, almost tripping in her strappy gold sandals.

The heat in the room enfolded them like a steaming blanket after the chill of the air outside. Rosemary felt her cheeks begin to burn. As she stood in the doorway next to Jonathan, who was still gripping her arm, she decided it was not only the heat which was turning her pale gold skin an unattractive shade of puce. Who did this virile ape beside her think he was, mauling her about like a sack of wholemeal flour? Her golden-brown eyes sparked angrily as she turned to face him—and Jonathan, glancing down at her, thought again what a captivating young woman his daughter's teacher was, even when she was flaming mad at him, as she very obvioulsy was at the moment, for no reason which he could understand. Until that car had blasted a promising interlude to the stars, Rosemary's responses to his kiss had been everything he could have wished for, and certainly *had* wished for quite fervently.

'Now what's the matter?' he asked mockingly, in a voice calculated to inflame her further.

'You are,' spat Rosemary. 'Don't you think it was bad enough forcing yourself on me just now, without topping it off by hauling me around by the hair? That caveman stuff doesn't impress me at all.'

Jonathan stared down at her unsmilingly, his dark eyebrows raised in disbelief. 'Come off it, pussy cat,' her replied, releasing her arm quickly. 'Let's face it, I didn't *have* to force myself on you. And I did *not* haul you by the hair, appealing as that idea is starting to become.' He paused, and the stern features relaxed perceptibly as a slow, reminiscent grin began to spread across his face. 'In fact, as I remember it, all I did was take you by the arm and draw you back into the warm cocoon of this blazing hot hotel.' He pulled out his handkerchief again and touched it to his still perspiring forehead. 'So please stop looking at me as if I'm some kind of monster, Miss Reid.'

So she was Miss Reid again. After a kiss like that. Rosemary edged away from him, afraid of what his nearness was doing to her senses.

'I didn't imagine you were a monster,' she replied coldly.

He smiled quizzically. 'No. Just a caveman.'

At that moment Alice appeared beside them, muttering

something about 'time out to cool off' because she didn't want her dog club being accused of scandalous behaviour behind the potted palms. Rosemary came to the conclusion that, apart from the fact that there wasn't a potted palm in sight, there was not much which got past Alice.

She watched as the white-haired little lady pulled Jonathan determinedly on to the dance-floor. Then she made her way back to her table. As the deaf old gentleman beside her rambled happily on about ears—he seemed to have a fixation on the subject—Rosemary's mind went back over the events of the evening.

Why *had* she reacted so perversely to Jonathan's kiss? Because he was right: she had indeed been willing, and there was really no denying that she found Jonathan Riordan quite breathtakingly attractive. But she was not yet ready to get involved with a man again. Not when that man was the father of her most difficult pupil, far too attractive to be safe—and obviously only looking for a passing affair with a woman who had briefly caught his fancy.

'Ears much too long,' barked the man next to her in a suddenly raised voice.

Rosemary jumped.

'Er—yes,' she agreed hastily. 'I'm sure you're quite right.'

'Course I am.' He nodded, and the persistent voice droned contentedly on again, convinced that his audience's attention was suitably riveted.

Watch it, my girl, thought Rosemary. Just remember Ronald.

Not long ago she had been sure that she would eventually marry Ronald. They had been going out for three years and marriage had seemed the obvious outcome. Then suddenly he had told her that he needed space to breathe, time to decide if they were really right for each other. At first she had been hurt and bewildered, but after a month or two she found that she was enjoying her freedom, and that life was much more fun without Ronald glowering at her if she even so much as spoke to another man. When, five months later, he told her that he had decided they should get back together, Rosemary was able to tell him, quite truthfully, that she was no longer interested.

A few months later she moved down to Vancouver.

That had been last summer, and she was completely detached about Ronald now. He didn't matter to her one way or the other. So why was she suddenly backing off from Jonathan—because she felt he wasn't safe? Was safety all she wanted? Watching him spin Alice deftly across the floor, Rosemary had a strong feeling that safety was the last thing she wanted at this moment. If she were honest with herself, what she really wanted was Jonathan—and quite suddenly she couldn't bear to watch him any longer.

With a hasty apology to the ear-man, she jumped up from her chair and ran into the ladies' room. It was unoccupied, and she leaned her head thankfully against the coldness of the mirror.

After a while she pulled herself upright and stared at her reflection. The light brown eyes staring back at her were wide and anxious, and there were faint traces of a frown between her brows. Quickly she smoothed out the lines, applied some lipstick and smiled. That was better.

With a restoration of her normally sunny countenance, it came to her that she knew exactly why Jonathan frightened her. It was because he had the power to hurt her, perhaps even more than Ronald had done—and she was not ready to be hurt again. Not yet. Maybe she never would be.

Straightening her shoulders, she marched back into the banquet-room, her smile plastered firmly on her lips.

'So you managed to escape the mouth,' murmured Jonathan approvingly, as Rosemary sat down beside him.

Her fixed smile disappeared at once and was replaced by a puzzled frown. 'What do you mean, the mouth? Oh, I see.' She nodded and the smile returned, this time with genuine amusement. 'Of course. You mean the mouth who had my ear—in more ways than one.'

A muscle twitched as the corner of Jonathan's mouth. 'Well put. And I see him heading this way again. Shall we escape to the dance-floor?'

Caught between the devil and the ear expert, Rosemary felt she had no choice. But she didn't really want to dance with Jonathan again. Such close proximity was too un-nerving—almost suffocating, in fact.

It took all the self-discipline she had to restrain the crazy urgings of her body and to maintain a discreet distance between herself and Jonathan as he led her around the floor. But she managed it.

'Now what the hell's wrong?' he demanded, after an unsuccessful attempt to draw her closer.

Rosemary, hearing the controlled frustration in his voice, gave him an aloof, cool little smile and didn't answer. Then, perversely, she was annoyed when he appeared to take her at face value and moved her a fraction further from his body.

Beast, she thought to herself. Anyway, one thing was certain. After tonight he would have no inclination to ask her out again. And that was exactly what she wanted—

wasn't it?'

Jonathan looked down at her little face and was almost but not quite convinced that the estimation he had formed of Rosemary Reid when he had first met her—prim, proper and self-righteous—was substantially correct. And when she spent the remainder of the evening treating him with brittle condescension, as if he were a small boy who didn't know how to behave, he found himself fighting a strong desire to take those slim shoulders in his hands and shake that smug smile from her lovely lips.

He didn't do it, though, and shortly after midnight he drove her and Alice back to Richmond. The atmosphere in the Lincoln was tired and tense, and Alice's eyes kept glancing between the two of them with an observant, bird-like perception. Nobody spoke much, and as soon as Jonathan pulled into Alice's driveway, Rosemary jumped out. She gave fulsome thanks to Alice for inviting her to a delightful evening, extended a cool nod to Jonathan to thank him for the ride, and with a quick, unnatural smile hurried away to her own home next door.

'Humph,' grunted Alice, staring after her. 'You should have left my nephew to his own devices, young man. Because I don't think all your machinations have done you one bit of good, have they?' She poked a finger accusingly at his chest as he helped her out of the car.

Jonathan, was also staring after Rosemary, had his head averted from her, so she could not see his expression, but when he replied, his voice was low and thoughtful, and very faintly amused.

'Oh, I don't know,' he said slowly. 'I think I may have done myself quite a bit of good, if Rosemary Reid is half the woman I think she is.'

'Hm. She's probably got more *sense* than you think she

has, young man. I can't see my Rosemary being taken in by—indigestion.' Alice made the last word sound like a thoroughly reprehensible affliction.

Jonathan choked, and put a hand quickly to his lips. 'I don't know,' he said again. 'I wouldn't be surprised to find that Miss Reid is just as susceptible as the next woman if she wants to be, and if one can ever get past her defences.'

In the kitchen of the house next door Rosemary was vigorously stirring a mug of instant coffee and thinking along much the same lines.

She was indeed beginning to berate herself for treating him so indifferently after he had kissed her with such passion by the swimming-pool. At the time, keeping him at a distance had seemed the sensible thing to do. But now she was alone in this warm, quiet kitchen with its utilitarian furniture bought cheaply and in a hurry, and she wished she had someone to talk to. Someone tall, tawny-blonde and handsome, with that slow, seductive smile that could melt all the barricades she had built around her heart.

No, she ordered herself firmly, pushing the coffee-cup away. You went through all that with Ronald. And Jonathan Riordan is the sort of man that women always fall for. The kind who invariably lead to heartache. She sighed, and wandered into the bedroom. Yes, Jonathan might be a fascinating, very sexy man, but he was also a manipulative schemer. Look at the way he had manoeuvred Derek into swapping places with him.

Right. She came to a decision. If he tried to see her again, she would tell him in no uncertain terms that he was wasting his time.

But when six days had passed without a word from

Jonathan, Rosemary began to think that even hoping,
without much confidence, that he was panting to see her
again had been the height of misguided arrogance.

Tamsin appeared in her classroom as usual on Monday
morning, and Rosemary had to overcome an embarrassing
tendency to flush and lower her eyes when she caught the
girl's eyes fixed on her in open, very curious speculation.
Did she know that her father had been out with her on
Saturday, then? If she did, she would probably resent it.

Throughout the day Tamsin's behaviour was
exemplary. On Tuesday it was the same. She put her
equipment away neatly and handed in homework that was
both legible and accurate.

This remarkable turnabout continued all week, and on
Friday, when Tamsin happened to be the last one in the
classroom after school, Rosemary called her over, smiled,
and told her how delighted she was with the improvement
in her work and behaviour.

Tamsin's strong jaw which so resembled her father's
had tilted belligerently when Rosemary had called her
name. Now it dropped quickly and she gave her teacher a
sweet, rather shy little smile in return.

'Do you mean I needn't leave your class?'

Rosemary's eyes widened. 'Of course you needn't.
Whatever gave you that idea?'

'Well, my Dad said I had to. And then he said he'd do
his best to see I didn't transfer. So I thought it might have
been your idea. That you *wanted* me to move.' She turned
her head away quickly and the beautiful soft brown hair
swung in a rippling cascade down her back.

'No, Tamsin, that was the last thing I wanted.'

'Oh.' Tamsin stared at the floor.

Rosemary watched her, puzzled. 'If you liked being in

my class why did you keep trying to cause trouble, Tamsin? Until this week, I mean.'

There was a long silence, and when Tamsin finally raised her head Rosemary saw that the familiar mutinous tilt to her jaw was back, and her strong mouth clamped tightly shut.

'Tamsin?' repeated Rosemary.

The girl's wide eyes filled suddenly with tears, and the defiant expression crumpled. 'I don't know,' she whispered. 'I think I wanted someone to—to . . .'

'Pay attention to you?'

Tamsin sniffed. 'Maybe. I don't know. I guess so.'

'But, Tamsin, we all pay attention to you. I'm sure your father does, too.'

'Yes, but my other teachers are men. So's my Dad.'

You can say that again, thought Rosemary with feeling. But she didn't say it. Instead she agreed cautiously, 'Yes, I suppose sometimes there must be things you would rather discuss with a woman. But your father must have women friends. I'm sure they're interested.'

'Not in me, they aren't. They're just interested in his money.'

Rosemary thought of Jonathan's magnificent physique and presence, and strongly doubted that. But the subject of Tamsin's father led to another train of thought.

'Tamsin,' she began hurriedly. 'I hope that this sudden change in behaviour—and of course I'm delighted about it—but what I mean is, I hope your father coming to see me hasn't caused you any—problems, at home.'

Tamsin's wide eyes flashed briefly, but the quick flare of indignation fizzled immediately into doubt. 'He didn't threaten to beat me into behaving, if that's what you mean,' she said dully. 'You must know that's not his style.'

Rosemary swallowed. Oh, lord. She didn't know much about Jonathan's style, but that hadn't been what she meant at all, had it? 'No, no, of course I didn't think that for a moment,' she said hastily. 'I just wondered if you're happy.'

'Why shouldn't I be?' replied Tamsin in a high, strained voice. She turned to her desk and began to gather up her books with a lot of slamming and slapping.

'No reason,' said Rosemary quickly. 'I just wondered.' Help. This was all coming out wrong. 'I'm glad everything's fine,' she added brightly. 'And, Tamsin, if you ever need someone to talk to—well, I'm always here.'

'Thanks,' muttered Tamsin, not looking at her. 'Thanks, Miss Reid.'

Rosemary opened her mouth to say more, but before she could gather her thoughts, Tamsin had slammed the door behind ther and was fleeing down the hall.

For a moment Rosemary stood immobile, gazing at the closed door. Then automatically she began to check the catches on the doors of the cages lining the walls.

Now what had all that been about? Did Tamsin's father neglect her? Was she just lonely? Perhaps they were both lonely. Or perhaps Tamsin knew about the dog-club dance and resented it . . .

She shook her head and threw her books and papers into the brand-new briefcase she had bought at the beginning of the week to prevent a repeat of last weekend's soggy mishap. A few minutes later she was hurrying out to the car park.

This Friday evening there was no tall figure lurking in the rain to detain her, and soon she was fighting the traffic over Knight Street Bridge to Richmond.

Murphy was waiting for her as she pulled into the driveway. His small, red body squirmed ecstatically and he gave little grunts of pleasure as he followed her into the kitchen and waited hopefully for the handout he was convinced was on its way to his ever-receptive mouth. When the phone rang before Rosemary could reach the cookie jar, his ears dropped dejectedly, and he fixed her with a look of baleful reproach.

She smiled at him and picked up the receiver. It was Henry Parkinson. 'How about coming to the pot-luck supper at my church tomorrow night?' he suggested cheerfully.

Good old kind, platonic Henry, who never harassed her or made the slightest attempt to turn their friendship into anything more than just that. Well, why not? From dog-club banquet to church supper, she thought wryly. Life was becoming a whirl of sophisticated activity. But, at any rate, Henry's church supper would be a far cry from the banquet which had turned into such a sexually charged affair last weekend. A *refreshing* change, she told herself firmly.

'Thanks very much,' she replied brightly. 'Of course I'd love to come.'

She hung up the phone and found a cookie for the portly and still hopeful Murphy. Supper with Henry would be all right. No surprises. Safe. Just exactly what she wanted.

Which made it all the more surprising that when the phone rang again at ten o'clock the next morning and Jonathan's deep, slow voice reverberated in her ear, Rosemary's thumping heart flipped over like a pancake. When he asked her if she felt like risking his company to-night for dinner, the shock of anticipation almost knocked her off her feet.

Until she remembered she was going out with Henry.

# CHAPTER FIVE

'I CAN'T,' said Rosemary baldly, discovering to her chagrin that for the moment she was quite incapable of giving him the perfectly reasonable explanationfor her refusal. She was having too much trouble catching her breath.

'Why not?' Jonathan was not willing to let her off the hook that easily.

Rosemary swallowed, clutched the phone more tightly in her mind and replied as calmly as she could, 'Because I have a previous engagement.'

'Hmm,' murmured Jonathan. 'Straight out of Emily Post's *Book of Etiquette.*'

Rosemary's breathing returned to normal and she gave an exasperated sigh. 'It happens to be true,' she snapped. 'I'm going to a church supper—with one of the teachers from school.'

Jonathan digested this information. 'I see,' he replied agreeably. 'In that case, I suppose dinner with me is out of the question.'

Rosemary noted that he had not asked the question which was none of his business—whether 'one of the teachers' happened to be male or female. Now she supposed he would say goodbye and hang up. She felt an unhappy sinking sensation in the pit of her stomach.

But he didn't hang up. Instead she heard the sound of a chair being pulled across the floor and then the faint creak of a body settling into it. She imagined him leaning backwards as he stretched out his long legs and settled his muscular thighs more comfortably in the chair.

'So,' he said, after a long pause, 'what are you doing now, then, Rosemary Reid?'

'Getting ready to take Alice's dogs for a walk on the dyke. She's driven out to Mission today to have a pow-wow with a fellow dog breeder. So I said I'd exercise the dogs.'

'*All* of them?' He sounded appalled.

'No, just Murphy and Muffin. The others are quite happy in their runs. M and M are house dogs, though.'

'Don't I know it. I made the mistake of sitting down while Alice and I were waiting for you last Saturday. The seat of my trousers was nicely matted with ginger.'

'Was it? Your jacket must have hidden it.'

There was a long silence during which Rosemary contemplated the interesting possibilities of Jonathan with a ginger-coloured behind. When the silence began to grow ridiculous, he said suddenly, 'How would you like company on your dog walk?'

'Whose?' asked Rosemary stupidly.

'Whose do you think? Mine, naturally.'

'Oh.' For once in her life, Rosemary was bereft of words.

'Well?' he persisted impatiently. 'Is the idea so abhorrent?'

'No—no, of course not. But—I'll be leaving in a minute.'

'Well, don't. I'll be there in half an hour. Wear your sexy red track-suit.'

'I don't have a sexy red track-suit.'

'Your hot pink one, then.' There was a teasing note

in his voice now.

'*Or* a hot pink one,' snapped Rosemary. 'I don't own a track-suit at all. I don't think they do much for my figure—or anyone else's for that matter.'

'Oh,' said Jonathan, who had rather fancied her figure in a track suit. 'That's too bad. See you in half an hour.'

Before Rosemary could reply, he had hung up the phone.

Half an hour later to the second, the green Lincoln sped across the bridge spanning the ditch in front of her house, and slammed to a stop beneath the living-room window. Rosemary gave herself a last quick appraisal in the bedroom mirror, patted her stomach and decided she looked quite presentable in the bulky blue sweater and jeans which she had peversely exchanged for the red sweater and slacks she had put on when she got up that morning. Pushing her soft fair hair nervously over her shoulder, she went to open the door.

Jonathan's spectacular body was emerging from the car with leisurely grace. Rosemary watched him stroll towards her with his hands in the pockets of his jeans, and an easy smile on his lips. Her mouth went suddenly dry, and she held on to the doorframe for suport. She had forgotten just how overwhelming he could be.

'I was wrong,' he said, running his eyes over her with frank approval. 'Blue is definitely your colour.'

'Thank you,' said Rosemary demurely, feeling instantly foolish for having changed her red outfit for no other reason than that she had not wanted him to think he could tell her what to wear.

She didn't tell him she thought that he looked marvellous too, in tight-fitting black jeans and a soft, strokable grey pullover.

Jonathan shook his head. 'You're a hard woman,' he told her severely. 'There I was, prepared to spend the morning reclining in glorious indolence on the sun-porch, anticipating a warm, wonderful evening, with a warm, wonderful woman—and what happens? I find myself rushing out to Richmond for what will un-doubtedly turn out to be an exhaustingly brisk walk in the wind—with two exhaustingly energetic dogs.'

'It was your idea,' replied Rosemary drily, refusing to be side-tracked by his flattering reference to the missed possibilities of the evening.

'No, it wasn't. My idea was a nice brisk sit.' His face looked so ridiculously woebegone that Rosemary started to laugh.

'In that case, help yourself to the couch,' she chuckled, waving at the cheerful, red-flowered piece which was just visible through the doorway. 'It may not be as exotic as your sun-porch, but it's really quite com-fortable.'

'My sun-porch is not in the least exotic,' replied Jonathan glumly. 'Not with the Whitehead clan next door. They start playing football at nine a.m. and by nine fifteen they're all shouting at each other. Some-where around nine forty-five I turn the radio up to drown them out, then they turn theirs up to drown me out, and my neighbour on the other side comes over to complain. I offer him him a beer, he accepts, and by noon the Whiteheads have gone out to create mayhem in the parks and my neighbour and I have had several more beers and gone peacefully to sleep. That's why it's relaxing—but it's certainly not exotic.'

Rosemary eyed him doubtfully, not sure whether to

believe him or not. His eyes were grey-green, smokey and completely without guile, but there was a slight tremor at the corner of his mouth, and she knew all too well how much he liked to tease.

'Nonsense,' she said repressively, refusing to laugh. 'You can't blame your laziness on the Whiteheads. On second thoughts, forget the couch. A nice, gale-force walk in exactly what you need. Come on.' She pulled the door shut behind her and without thinking grabbed his hand and tried to tow him up the driveway. He didn't move.

Suddenly conscious of his hand, which had shifted imperceptibly and was now holding on to hers, she turned slowly around.

He was looking down at her with an odd, enigmatic expression in those formidable eyes, and she felt shaken, scared almost, and irresistibly drawn to him. She took a step forward. His grip tightened, and she dropped her eyes to stare down at their clasped hands. Then she made a small, half inaudible sound, like the whimper of a small animal, and tried to pull away.

Jonathan didn't let go, but he smiled at her, an amused, understanding smile, and said quietly, 'OK, Rosemary Reid. Lead the way to the dogs.'

Rosemary smiled shakily back, nodded and moved towards the low shrubs separating Alice's property from her own. Jonathan followed her willingly. But he still held on to her hand.

When they reached Alice's front door he released his grip, and she scrabbled in the tight pocket of her jeans for the key, wishing that he wasn't watching her efforts so closely, and with that irritating grin on his lips.

As soon as the door opened, two ginger-brown bodies

came tumbling down the steps, barking and snuffling happily at their liberators' feet.

'Do you like dogs?' asked Rosmary, as Jonathan bent to scratch Muffin behind the ear.

'Sure. Provided they're someone else's responsibility. Tamsin wants a dog,' he added offhandedly.

Rosemary glanced at him, and moved Murphy's nose from her pocket. 'Perhaps she should have one. Sometimes she seems a lonely little girl.'

'Not so little. And as you told me rather forcibly, not at all responsible. If I got her a dog, I'd be the one stuck to look after it, not Tamsin.'

'I'm not so sure. Maybe if she had something to love and look after, it might make her happier and she might grow up a bit, learn to think of others.'

'She can love and look after me,' said Jonathan roughly. 'Come on. If we *have* to walk these animated carpets, for heaven's sake, let's get on with it.' He began to stride across the grass.

Rosemary stared after him, exasperated, but still unable to suppress a surge of admiration for the lithe body moving away from her with such heart-stopping, totally unconscious sensuality. So he didn't like being given advice about his daughter. Well, if anyone knew that, she should. But it was yet another reason why she would be much better off, more sensible, not to let herself become involved with this vital, fascinating, but very dangerous man. Dangerous to her peace of mind, in any case. She frowned and started to follow him across the grass.

A few minutes later they were seated side by side in the Toyota. Jonathan's long legs almost touched the dashboard, and he looked alarmingly big within the confined space of Rosemary's small car. The dogs were snuffling excitedly in the back as she turned on to Westminster Highway to drive towards her favourite part of the dyke.

'You took that corner too fast,' remarked Jonathan, not sounding as if he minded.

'I did not,' snapped Rosemary indignantly.

He shrugged and didn't pursue the subject. But Rosemary, seeing the superior smile playing across his mouth, felt an immediate urge to wipe it off his face.

Deliberately she swerved into the oncoming lane. His lips tightened slightly, but otherwise he made no sign that he had noticed. Beast, she thought. He won't give me the satisfaction of even that small revenge.

Instead he leaned over the back seat and started to make senseless conversation to the dogs.

*Men,* she thought disgustedly. Then Murphy responded to a comment about rabbits by planting a long, wet kiss across Jonathan's superior nose.

'Well done, boy,' she murmured, as he drew back with a startled grimace to wipe the damp evidence of the dog's affection from his face.

'Thanks,' he taunted. 'Your sympathy is greatly appreciated.'

Rosemary drew the car to the edge of dyke with a flourish. When they got out, there was just one inch to spare between the right wheels and disaster.

Jonathan raised his eyebrows. 'And you're supposed to be an inspiration to the young,' he gibed.

'Well, I might be, if you weren't such an inspiration to insanity,' she snapped, and was feeling a little embarrassed that she had risked her precious car for no better reason than to aggravate Jonathan Riordan.

And it hadn't worked, either, because he was standing with his hands in his pockets watching her, his tawny head bright against the sky and that maddening grin still on his lips.

Irritably she pulled the back door open, and two furry forms bounded across the turf and on to the sturdy wooden bridge across the dyke.

Jonathan stared after them disapprovingly. 'I knew they'd be deplorably energetic,' he muttered.

'It's not deplorable at all. It's healthy,' retorted Rosemary, pursing her lips and looking virtuous.

'Oh, God.' Jonathan groaned. 'I knew it. You're one of those revoltingly hearty people who jog twice a day, eat brown rice and lentils and keep on telling the rest of us we shouldn't smoke or drink.'

Rosemary stopped trying to look virtuous and laughed. 'No, I'm one of those revoltingly ordinary people who walk dogs. And if we don't get a move on there won't be much walking about it because we'll need roller skates just to catch up to that pair.'

Jonathan sighed, but his arm slipped around her waist and he begun to propel her swiftly after the dogs, who were frisking about in the boggy marshland beyond the dyke which bordered the mighty Fraser River. Far out on the horizon the misty shapes of the Gulf Island loomed softly through the haze. Closer to hand the white sails of a pleasure boat gleamed sharply in the sun. It was a bright, warm day for March, and would have been quite balmy without the wind that almost always blew across the dyke.

'You can see Vancouver Island sometimes, when it's very clear,' remarked Rosemary, disturbingly conscious of his arm around her waist and the hand which had curved loosely over her hip.

'I know. I grew up here.'

'In Richmond?'

'No, in Vancouver, but my brother and I often used to come out here to go frog-hunting. There were more ditches in those days. Now they've filled most of them in to widen the roads.'

'Mm,' murmured Rosémary, unbearably distracted by the feel of his hand on her hip. 'I suppose they have. I didn't know you had a brother.'

'And a sister, but they both moved east years ago, along with my parents, so Tamsin and I are on our own.'

'Yes, I see. By the way, about Tamsin. She's behaving much better this week. It's almost as if she's scared of something.' She glanced up at him provocatively. 'But she assures me you don't beat her.'

Jonathan saw the golden lights dancing in her eyes and muttered something about there being plenty of time to change that, and she needn't think Tamsin would be the recipient.

'Are you sure you could summon up the energy?' she asked drily. 'I mean, for someone who finds walking so deplorably strenuous . . .'

'I think I might just manage it.' His voice was deep, and vibrant with suppressed laughter. His hand was stroking her thigh now, and little sensual shivers were running up her spine and destroying all hope of intelligent conversation. But she did want to talk about Tamsin, and now was as good a time as any. Besides, Jonathan's nearness unnerved her. She pushed his arm away and moved quickly to the edge of the gravelled path.

'Your daughter,' she said firmly, trying to look sensible and intelligent, and hoping he wouldn't notice the heightened colour in her cheeks.

He grinned, and Rosemary's heart turned over again. 'Yes? My daughter. Is there a problem?' His eyebrows lifted lazily, and she felt a familiar urge to hit him.

'No,' she said, 'not any more. But I *am* worried about her. This sudden change in behaviour isn't normal.'

They were standing across from each other now and the dogs were chasing birds along the dyke. A track-suited jogger panted past, eyes staring ahead in agonised concentration.

Jonathan looked after him and shook his head, but when he turned back to Rosemary his expression was quite sober.

'It's entirely normal for Tamsin,' he told her flatly. 'I suppose she's at an awkward age, and the thing you can predict about my daughter is that she'll be unpredictable.'

'Yes, but I still don't understand . . .'

'There may not be much to understand, Rosemary. I do my best, but the nature of my business takes me away a lot—and I know she sometimes resents that.' His grey eyes turned opaque, suddenly hard to interpret as he stared at the black-tipped wings of a heron flying low above the marsh, its long legs tucked gracefully behind it. 'Of course Mrs Peacock is there during the week, but I don't think Tamsin likes her much.'

'Then why not replace her?'

'For God's sake, Rosemary! She's a perfectly competent housekeeper most of the time. I'm not about to get rid of the woman at the whim of a tiresome teen-ager.'

Rosemary felt a quick flash of sympathy for Tamsin. Of course Jonathan did his best, but a man with a business to run, and, and strains and pressures of his own, with no wife to care for his daughter and no one to share the domestic load, must have often found it hard to understand that the awkward adolescent also had pressures of her own.

She stopped, and scuffed her toe in the gravel, stirring up a small cloud of dust.

'I suppose it *is* difficult, she said tentatively. 'And I suppose I was right in the first place. Tamsin's behaviour was just a bid for attention—even unfavourable attention.'

'Quite possibly.' Jonathan's tone was curt, and he started to move quickly after the dogs.

But Rosemary was unwilling to leave it at that. 'Why do you think she's suddenly changed her tactics?' she asked, running to catch him up.

He didn't look at her, but strode on with his hands in his pockets. 'If you must know, I imagine Tamsin has always liked you. She just didn't know how to show it. Then I made the mistake of telling her I'd been out with you, and she started to make plans.'

'Plans?'

'Mm. She's had a bee in her bonnet lately.' He still wasn't looking at her, and his eyes were fixed rigidly on the horizon. 'She's got some mad idea that I ought to get married again.'

'Oh,' said Rosemary, not knowing what to reply.

He glanced at her quickly, and then looked away again. 'Yes. I don't know why it's suddenly become a campaign on her part, but she's suggested it several times.' His mouth twisted wryly. 'Not that she has ever approved of anyone I went out with. Except, just possibly—you. That, my dear Rosemary, could explain the changed in her behaviour. She may hope you're going to be her stepmother.'

When Rosemary looked at his face, she saw that here was a sardonic little smile pulling at the edge of his lips.

'Good grief,' she said awkwardly, trying to digest this surprising information. 'Well, I suppose that makes some sort of sense.'

'Not a great deal. But I can't seem to convince her that I have no intention of marrying again.'

'Haven't you?' Rosemary hesitated, then added almost involuntarily, 'Why not?'

As soon as she said it she knew she shouldn't have asked. And she was right. Irritation—mixed with something else, something bleak and withdrawn—flashed momentarily in his eyes, and his lips were suddenly hard.

'Because I tried it once,' he replied harshly, 'and it's not an experiment I want to repeat. Why? Were you thinking of proposing yourself as a candidate?'

Rosemary gasped. A hot surge of indignation flamed through her and her fists clenched furiously at her sides as she took a step towards him.

'Oh!' she spat, through lips that were pulled taut with anger as she realised that her orginal feelings about his personality had been absolutely right. 'Oh! Of all the incredibly conceited, arrogant, self-satisfied, vain, rude, overbearing, supercilious, pompous . . .'

As she spoke, the withdrawn look had gradually faded from his eyes, and he passed a hand quickly across his mouth. 'Did you say pompous?'

Rosemary almost ground her teeth. 'Yes,' she hissed,

'and impossible and insulting and . . .'

'Whoa!' Jonathan held up his hand. 'You do have a way with words, Rosemary Reid, but before you've exhausted the entire dictionary . . .' He smiled placatingly. 'May I offer an apology? Another one. I shouldn't have said that.'

'No, you should not,' snapped Rosemary, her eyes still flashing sparks.

'I know, but you see . . .' He spread his arms and shrugged, his eyes registering a kind of rueful regret. 'You see, I've run into so many women who hear wedding bells the moment I come near them—Tamsin calls them gold-diggers—and—well, I just wanted to make my position clear.' He paused, and the regretful expression changed to one of teasing admiration. 'Did anyone ever tell you you look lovely when you're angry?'

'Frequently,' replied Rosemary scathingly. 'It's a very unoriginal line. And if you call that piece of chauvinistic boasting an apology . . .'

'I don't,' said Jonathan immediately. 'You're absolutely right. It was inexcusable. You've given me no reason whatever to imagine you're lusting to marry me.' He held out his hand. 'Come on. Shall we call it a truce? Those dogs of yours are fast disapprearing over the horizon.'

Rosemary eyed him sideways, only partly mollified. She ignored the hand. His choice of words was provocative. Marriage was certainly not on her mind, but lust—lust was something else.

She fell into step beside him as they hurried after the dogs, maintaining an uneasy silence. Yet it was impossible to walk beside Jonathan, watching the tall, athletic body move with such casual virility in the tight jeans and soft, oh-so-strokable pullover, without feeling the stirrings of something which was certainly not platonic. But, really, his remarks about marriage were totally uncalled for. Why had he reacted so strongly? She shook her head in bewilderment, and glancing up at his profile, saw it etched clean and strong against the sky.

There was something very oldd about Jonathan's attitude, she decided, watching him covertly as he drew back his arm to throw a stick for the dogs. Murphy and Muffin scampered after it with tumbling enthusiasm, and Rosemary thought, not for the first time, that for someone who professed to be opposed to all forms of exercise, Jonathan was a superbly vigorous specimen of mouth-watering masculinity. And it was probably true about all those women hearing wedding bells.

She frowned, and felt the stirrings of something which she was damned if she was going to acknowledge was jealously.

Far ahead of them the dogs, still in pursuit of the stick, drew to a skidding halt as a little black and white mongrel hopped across a bridge and came charging furiously at them with ears flying wide and teeth ferociously bared. A moment later three furry bodies became one growling, snapping ball of enthusiastic warfare.

Jonathan swore, and started to run towards the mêlée. As Rosemary ran after him she was struck again by his extraordinary virility. By the time she caught up to him he had Murphy and Muffin firmly by the collars and the little mongrel was hurtling back over the bridge as if all the tollers in Canada were after him—armed to the teeth and lusting hungrily for blood.

'How did you manage that?' asked Rosemary, in laughing admiration. All her resentment had faded now and she watched as he straightened his body slowly, telling the dogs in no uncertain terms to 'sit'. They sat. 'Last time I got into a dogfight,' she went on, 'I ended up as bloody as the combatants.'

'Well, I'm not exactly unscathed myself,' replied Jonathan, grinning down at her. 'See.' He held out his arm and she saw that his muscular forearm sported several toothmarks.

'Oh, dear,' she murmured. 'Still, it could be much worse, couldn't it? You did very well.'

'Experience,' smiled Jonathan. 'When I was a kid we had a labrador cross who doubled as a shark. My brother and I spent half our lives rescuing the neighbourhood pooches from his jaws. His great ambition, fortunately never fulfilled, was to devour our inoffensive postman.'

'Really? What happened to him in the end?'

'I'm afraid he ate one of the neighbourhood kids and we had to get rid of him.' His eyes glazed over and he added reminiscently, 'He was precisely the sort of kid I would have eaten myself if I'd been a dog. But there you are. Neighbours don't like it.'

His eyes turned back to Rosemary, and she started to laugh.

'Compared to that pugilistic monster, these two miscreants must seem positive amateurs.'

'Believe me, they are.'

All antagonism gone, they turned to stroll along the dyke again, watching the wind ripple the grass, and flocks of small birds flit jauntily across the sky. Jonathan's arm slipped round her waist, and now it felt right—as though that was somehow where it belonged.

Far out over the water they heard the honking of the snow geese, and then clouds of the beautiful white birds appeared outlined in silver against the grey horizon. They both stopped to gaze in awe as the cloud came noisily to rest on the foreshore, turning into a white, restless sea of wings and feathers, shifting and stirring beside the shimmering river.

'I love the snow geese,' whispered Rosemary. 'This is my favourite time of the year.'

'I'm beginning to think it's mine,' agreed Jonathan, watching the wind lift the soft hair from her shoulders, and thinking that any time of year would be his favourite if that time and space happened to hold Rosemary. She was having a very disturbing effect on him, this woman who wasn't one of his gold-diggers . . .

He shook his head, and mentally shook himself. Rosemary was a lovely young woman and he hoped he would see more of her. But not for a moment must he consider becoming seriously involved. He had discovered long ago where that could lead.

In the past it had led to Janet, and to her tragic, lonely dying. And never again would he allow any woman to become a serious factor in his life.

Especially not Rosemary Reid.

# CHAPTER SIX

ROSEMARY glanced at her watch. 'We should be getting back,' she remarked regretfully. 'I still have some shopping to do, and then I must get ready to go out.'

'To your church supper? Very commendable of you.' Jonathan nodded down at her with such an air of sanctimonious approval that Rosemary started to laugh.

She had laughed a lot this past hour. She had told Jonathan something about the trials and tribulations of teaching, and he had responded by telling her of his beginnings in the mining industry. First, he said, he had worked as a prospector in the field, and then, after taking a degree, as a geologist for the same company. Eventually he had become a professional engineer and made some risky but highly successful investments based on inside knowledge and, Rosemary suspected, sheer guts. Then he had sold out again at a handsome profit. Not long after that he and Derek had gone into partnership together.

None of it was particularly funny, but both of them found themselves laughing, and when Rosemary looked at her watch and discovered that it was time to leave she was genuinely surprised.

As the Toyota swerved into the driveway, Jonathan put his arm along the back of the seat and turned to face her.

'I'll be out of town for the rest of the week,' he told

her. 'But do you think you could avoid church suppers next Saturday—and the one after—and come out with me instead?'

Rosemary smiled. 'Thank you. Next Saturday will be fine. But I'm afraid I can't make the one after that. I'm taking fifteen students on a field trip to Long Beach that weekend.'

'By yourself?' he responded, with mock horror. 'What a horrifying prospect.'

'No, not by myself. Henry's coming. He's the one I'm going to the church supper with.' She glanced at him quickly and was inordinately pleased to note the slightest stiffening of his jaw. 'And John, our lab assistant, is coming too,' she added. 'So we'll be quite well staffed.'

'With fifteen kids? I doubt it.'

'Tamsin's one of them. She just asked me this week if she could come, and her behaviour has improved so much that I said yes. Didn't you know?'

'Mm?' He lifted his head, a faintly abstracted look in his eyes. His hand began to play absently with her hair, which hung down over the seat. 'Oh. Yes. I suppose she did mention it, but I'd forgotten.'

Rosemary wondered how he could forget that his only child, and the only other permanent occupant of his house, would be away for an entire weekend. But parents were an odd lot. Six years of teaching had taught her that, if nothing else.

His hand was stroking the back of her neck now, and she gave a little shiver.

'Cold?' he asked softly.

'Yes—no. Not really.'

'Not sure? Come here, then. I'll make up your mind for you.' His arm tightened around her shoulders and he pulled her slowly to face him. His head was very close to hers and she could see the pores of his skin and smell the faint, wonderfully masculine scent of his body. When his fingers curved behind her neck, her lips parted involuntarily—and then his mouth was on hers, his tongue against her teeth, probing her mouth in erotic exploration. His body shifted along the seat and she felt the pressure of his broad chest against her breasts as his other hand moved softly, sensuously down her body, and came to rest on her thigh.

Rosemary gave a little gasp, and put both arms around his neck, her fingers tangling fiercely in the springy strength of his hair. She was floating on a golden cloud of desire and the pounding warmth of her blood was like nothing she had ever known before.

'Jonathan . . .' she murmured, tearing her mouth from his. 'Jonathan . . .'

But whatever she had been going to say was never uttered, because at that moment Murphy decided he had enough of this enforced captivity and of the extraordinary antics on the seat in front of him. He put both paws up on Jonathan's shoulder, whimpered, and delivered a long, very thorough kiss behind his ear.

'God,' yelled Jonathan, releasing Rosemary so quickly that she almost hit her head against the door. 'What the hell . . . Oh, it's you.' He gave Murphy a forceful shove and sank back against the seat.

As Rosemary's breathing steadied, she raised her eyes from the corded sinews of his neck which showed invitingly above his sweater, and stared up into his face. It held an expression of such comical indignation that she started to laugh again—and once she started she couldn't stop.

Jonathan stared at her stonily, then gradually his mouth relaxed into a grin. 'Bloody dog,' he muttered at Murphy. 'You just ruined a perfectly promising seduction.'

'Like hell he did,' responded Rosemary, still laughing. When at last she had recovered from her hilarity, she saw that he was studying her with an odd, considering look in his eyes. 'I think,' he said slowly, stroking the back of her neck with his thumb,' I think I had better come with you on that jaunt to Long Beach the weekend after next. Just to keep you out of trouble.'

Rosemary gaped at him and, without knowing why, drew as far away from him as she could.

'Wh-what—why?' She was stumbling over her words like the class mouse being asked out by the captain of the football team. What was the matter with her?

'Is the idea so unpalatable?' he asked drily.

'No—no . . .' She was still doing it. Rosemary took a deep breath. 'It's just that—I'd rather you didn't. I—I mean we have enough staff already.' She swallowed uncomfortably, feeling more like a mouse then ever. 'Thank you for offering, though.'

Jonathan stared down at her with a slight furrow between his brows, and his grey eyes were very still. 'I see,' he said carefully, in a voice grown suddenly hard. 'With fifteen active kids on your hands, the three of you can't use an extra body—at least, not if it happens to be mine.'

Rosemary was irritated, partly with herself because the thought of a whole weekend spent in Jonathan's company had all of a sudden been too overwhelming to contemplate, and partly with him for not understanding.

'It's not that,' she mumbled, 'but this trip has already—already been organised. And we're all used to this sort of thing. You're not. I—we don't need you, you see, and—I don't want you to come.'

He stared at her, his face without expression. 'Right,' he said finally, in a voice that was harder than ever. 'That's clear enough then, isn't it?'

'No, you don't understand,' began Rosemary desperately, knowing that her inept and ungracious explanation had only made things worst. And, at some deeper level, she also knew it was her rejection of him as a man that had turned him into this harsh, withdrawn stranger—not the fact that she had denied him the dubious pleasure of a field trip with fifteen teenagers. Nobody in his right mind would regret that.

She glanced up at him doubtfully, and saw only steel and ice reflected in his eyes. And suddenly she had to get away. 'I really must go in now, I'm afraid,' she muttered, not looking at him. 'Will I still see you next Saturday?'

'Of course. If you still want to come. I don't make offers I don't intend to honour.'

Oh, dear. Now he sounded impossibly stuffy. 'If you'd rather not . . .' she began hopelessly.

'Miss Reid, if *you* would rather not,' said Jonathan curtly, 'you know you have only to say so. Otherwise I'll pick you up on Saturday at seven.'

Without looking at her again he flung open the door of the car, swung his legs on to the driveway and strode rapidly over to the Lincoln. Every line of his body was taut and rigid. Like a receding glacier, thought Rosemary unhappily as he slammed the door shut behind him and skidded much too quickly down the driveway.

'Come on, dogs,' she said glumly to the ginger-coloured furballs in the back. She opened the door to release them. 'I sure blew that one, didn't I?'

Murphy and Muffin only wagged agreeably and padded

off to their home next door. Rosemary let them in and trailed gloomily back to her own house, which now seemed more utilitarian and empty than ever. She glanced round absently. She must really get a few pictures soon, buy some pretty cushions, do something to make her house into a proper home.

But in her heart she knew that furniture had nothing to do with the feeling of hollow abandonment she was experiencing now. It was only Jonathan Riordan who could dispel that feeling—and he had left her in anger and would probably spend the evening with some gorgeous piece of cheesecake. One of his gold-diggers, I suppose, she sneered nastily to herself.

And the thought was no consolation at all.

Damn! She kicked irritably at an inoffensive pair of shoes, and began to get ready to go out.

The church supper with Henry was innocuous enough, but she was in such a mood of disgruntled confusion, a lot of it directed at herself, that she was unable to enjoy the friendly, unsophisticated occasion as she might have tried to do under other circumstances. But Henry was his usual undemanding self, and seemed not to mind that her thoughts were obviously elsewhere.

By Monday morning she was beginning to recover from her fit of depression and to look forward to Saturday, when she would see Jonathan again and, with any luck, put everything right between them. She tried hard not to think about the fact that she had shied away from him last weekend precisely because she wanted to avoid involvement—to hang on to the freedom she had found so attractive after the years with Ronald. She also tried to avoid thinking about Jonathan's equal determination to remain single and fancy-free.

Tamsin stayed after school that day to help her clean the cages, and Rosemary could not resist the temptation of asking a question that had, ridiculously, been gnawing at her for two days.

'Does you father really spend his Saturday mornings drinking beer and sleeping?' she enquired in a muffled voice—mindful of what Jonathan had said about Tamsin regarding her as a possible stepmother and knowing she should not be discussing him with his daughter.

Tamsin put down a bag of wood chips and gaped at her. 'Did he really tell you that?' she gasped. Then she started to giggle. 'Oh, I bet he did.'

'Yes,' agreed Rosemary, colouring slightly. 'He did.'

'Oh, dear.' Tamsin controlled herself with an effort. 'He is awful, isn't he? When he's in a good mood. No, he doesn't spend Saturdays sleeping. Sometimes he takes the company Cessna and has a look at some claims. He likes to keep an eye on things. And it's fun because I can go with him.'

'Oh,' said Rosemary grimly. 'So he's a flier, is he?'

'Oh, yes. And then other times he goes hang-gliding.' She grinned. 'I don't think he even drinks beer.'

It was Rosemary's turn to gape. 'Hang-gliding?'she exclamed. 'Did you say hang-gliding?'

'Yes, mostly around Grouse Mountain. He says he's going to let me do it one day. I often go to watch.'

Rosemary shook her head. Beer and sleep, he had said. When she saw him again, she would have a very large bone to pick with Tamsin's beguiling father.

Saturday morning rolled around surprisingly quickly, and she awoke with a feeling of expectation. She spent half the afternoon trying on different combinations of clothing, one minute dressing casually in slacks and a silk blouse so that Jonathan would think she was not over-impressed with his company, the next wearing low-cut, slinky black, so that he *would* be impressed with hers. In the end she settled for a soft blue jersey dress shot through with subdued threads of silver. She knew it clung to every graceful curve of her body, and that the plunging V-style neckline stopped just this side of indecency.

But when Jonathan arrived, looking magnificent in a superbly cut dark suit and white shirt which accentuated the clean lines of his jaw, his eyes played over her with cool appraisal, and she felt as if she were a teenager who should have known better than to ape her elders. Any minute now he would tell her to go and change into something more suitable to her age. Why did this man have such a talent for making her feel like one of her own students?

'Very seductive,' he remarked impassively. 'Shall we go?' So he had not forgiven her for her rejection of the week before. She supposed she couldn't blame him.

The restaurant Jonathan chose rose thirty floors into the sky above Vancouver, and if it had not been raining they would have had an impressive view of the city and its surrounding mountains, and of the lights flickering in the waters in the Inlet. As it was, the view was obscured by the pelting rain streaking against the heavy panes of glass, and the uncooperative weather did nothing to alleviate the atmosphere of grim reserve with which they had begun the evening.

To do him justice, Jonathan behaved with perfect attentiveness to her needs. In the elevator on the way up, he saw that she was gripping the handrail with white-faced dedication.

'What is it?' he asked quietly. 'Are you claustrophobic?'

Rosemary nodded dumbly. 'I'm afraid I am a little,' she murmured apologetically, feeling childish and thoroughly silly.

Without a word, Jonathan put his arm around her shoulders and held her firmly against his side. Just as they reached the top, she began to relax and her head came to rest against his arm. He glanced down at her enigmatically—but the moment the door opened he removed his support abruptly.

When Rosemary couldn't make up her mind what to order, Jonathan selected the most exotic items on the menu for her delectation. A seafood combination which melted in her mouth, followed by pheasant, which she was not at all sure that she appreciated.

Seeing her doubtfully expression, he asked her if anything was wrong.

'No. No.' She shook her head quickly, taking a hasty bite of her meal. 'It's delicious.'

She couldn't bring herself to tell him that for some reason the pheasant reminded her of the snow geese on the dyke.

Jonathan noted her discomfort, but she said nothing. If she wouldn't tell him what was troubling her, she would have to make the best of it on her own.

When the meal was over he ordered the most warmly mysterious coffee she had ever tasted and, by the time they had finished, her head was swirling pleasantly. She smiled across at him, all too aware that in spite of his attentiveness, and the flow of idle conversation he had kept up throughout the evening, he was as withdrawn and hard as he had been the first day in her classroom.

They did not recapture the laughter they had shared on the dyke. And she never did mention the hang-gliding or flying.

He returned her smile, but it was only a superficial stretching of the lips.

'I expect you'd like to go home now,' he suggested a few minutes later, as the last drop of coffee disappeared and the strain between them became positively oppressive.

She nodded jerkily. 'Yes. Yes, thank you, I expect that would be best.' There was no way she was going to break through that barrier of civility tonight.

And things would not be put right between them.

When he dropped her off, she asked him half-heartedly if he wanted to come in. He thanked her politely and refused. Rosemary held out her hand.

'Well, goodbye, then. And thank you for a lovely evening.'

'My pleasure.' He took her hand gravely, and held on to it for a long moment. His eyes locked with hers and there was something bleak and indecipherable in their smokey depths. Just for a second, she thought he was going to kiss her. Then she knew she must have mistaken the way his body had seemed to bend towards her, because his lips stiffened perceptibly, and he released her hand as if she had suddenly developed purple scales.

Rosemary turned away from him and walked into the house.

Jonathan watched her trail slowly up the steps, and fought down a barely controllable urge to follow her, to spin the willowy body into his arms and cover that luscious mouth with kisses. He had been thinking about just that all week. But somehow, when he had seen her waiting to greet him, looking cool and blue and aloof, he had been reminded forcibly of the way she had told him last week that he wasn't needed, that she—and John and

Henry—could manage quite well without him. And *that,* he recollected, was exactly the way he wanted her to feel.

But when he remembered again that supercilious tilt to her nose and the golden-brown eyes refusing to meet his, he wished the evening had not degenerated into an exercise in polite civility.

Then he rememberd Janet, and was glad it had.

Rosemary did not have much time to brood over the abortive evening with Jonathan, because the following week was spent in chaotic last-minute preparations for the field trip. She dealt with anxious parents who wanted to be sure that Charolotte would wear her warm boots outside because she was susceptible to colds, that Kevin would take his allergy medicine, and that Debbie would phone home at least once to let her parents know she had arrived safely. There was also a call from Janey Thatcher's mother asking if Colin Williams was going on the trip. When she was told he was, she requested the staff, obliquely, to ensure that Janey did not return home pregnant. Rosemary was devoutly thankful that Henry had fielded that call.

They were scheduled to leave on Friday morning. On Thursday evening Rosemary was relaxing with scrambled eggs and the paper when the telephone rang. It was Henry.

John had gone down with acute appendicitis and would not be able to come with them to Long Beach.

Appendicitis again, thought Rosemary digustedly. Only this time there was no chance it would turn conveniently into indigestion.

'What do we do now?' asked Henry, as the silence on the end of the line stretched on—and on.

'I don't know. Have you tried any of the other staff?'

'All of them.' Henry's voice had lost its usual buoyancy and he sounded almost panic-stricken.

'Oh.' She thought for a moment. 'We have to get someone, you know. We can't cope by ourselves. Besides, I doubt if the School Board would allow it.'

'So do I. Doubt it, I mean.'

Rosemary thought some more, her mind darting frantically in all directions in an effort to escape the obvious solution. She and Henry could try to manage on their own. Unthinkable. Or they could cancel the trip. But the students woud be devastated. And Tamsin would tell her father than it had been cancelled because they were short-staffed—and he would *know*—know that she was afraid to spend a weekend in his company. Or worse, he would think she found that company so unpleasant that she was willing to disappoint fifteen kids to avoid it.

No. She couldn't face that.

'I think I can get someone,' Rosemary told Henry at last. 'I'll call you back.' She hung up the phone abruptly.

Damn, she thought, staring balefully at a dent in the top of the white arborite table. She stretched out her hand and began to circle it absently with her thumb. But there was really no alternative, was there? No alternative at all.

Reluctantly, she reached for the phone.

And it rang six times before he answered.

# CHAPTER SEVEN

'YES. Hello.' His voice was gruff, and Rosemary had a sudden intuition that she had woken him up. Oh, lord, this wasn't going to be easy.

'Jonathan?' She tried to sound detached and non-committal.

There was dead silence on the other end of the line and then, faintly, Rosemary heard the sound of breathing rapidly exhaling.

'Yes. This is Jonathan Riordan.' The words were equally non-committal.

Rosemary groaned inwardly and forced herself to go on.

'It's Rosemary, Jonathan.'

'Yes, I know.'

He was not going to help her at all. She curled her fingers firmly around the back of her chair, moved the telephone from the counter on to the table, and began again.

'Jonathan, I have to ask you for a favour. A big favour.'

'Yes?' Still no encouragement, but at least he sounded awake now.

'Did I wake you up?' she asked, backing from the inevitable moment when she would have to explain the reason for her call.

'You did. Derek's away. He's followed Bozo to

Zimbabwe, and I've had a helluva day dealing with five disgruntled prospectors, one over-enthusiastic one, several very demanding clients—and Tamsin's new ferret. Sleep seemed the only escape.'

'Oh,' said Rosemary, wondering if she believed him. 'Did you say Tamsin had a ferret?'

'I did. And I suppose you *would* find that more arresting than the traumas of my executive work-day. Yes, Tamsin has a ferret. It was a compromise. There's no one here all day to take care of a dog, so I thought she might be satisfied with a ferret—to love and look after. Wasn't that how you put it?'

So he had listened to her, after all, and there was a definite edge to his voice. Rosemary took a firmer grip on the phone. 'I suppose it was. And—is everything working out well?'

'From the ferret's point of view, I suppose it is. So far she's bitten three of Tamsin's fingers, my chin and both my ears. And when Mrs Whitehead came over from next door to inspect her, she headed straight for the jugular.'

'Oh, dear.' Rosemary hesitated. 'And you going to keep her?'

'I'm very much afraid we are. Tamsin think she's wonderful, and seems to regard the continued survival of her fingers as irrelevant.'

'Oh, dear,' said Rosemary again. 'What do you call her?'

'Dracula.'

He pronounced the name with such grim disgust that Rosemary burst out laughing. When she realised there was no answering laughter at the other end, she controlled herself hastily and changed the subject.

'About that favour,' she pressed on reluctantly.

'Yes?'

They were back where they had started.

'Will you—would you . . Oh hell!'

'Will I would I what? Did you say "go to hell"? Because if that's what you woke me up for . . .'

'No. No, I didn't. Actually I'm trying to ask you if your offer still stands.' There. She had got it out.

'What offer?'

Oh, damn and blast the man, he was determined to make this as difficult as possible. She took a long breath. 'Your offer to help out this weekend.'

'Ah. That offer.' He was silent for so long that Rosemary wondered if he had left the phone. She was about to say something, when his voice came back across the wires. 'I understood I wasn't needed. And don't you think this is rather short notice? After all, I do have a business to run and, as I said, my partner is in Zimbabwe.'

'Oh. Yes, or course. I guess that makes it impossible, doesn't it? I'm sorry abou the notice, but our lab assistant just went down with appendicitis.'

'Appendicitis?' For the first time, she heard a certain lightening in his tone.

'Mm. That particular complaint does seem to follow me around, doesn't it? But of course, if Derek's away . . .'

'I didn't say I couldn't come. My assistant can handle things for one day. I just said it was short notice. Particulary when I was told before that you didn't want me . . . that the capable Miss Reid could manage much better on her own.'

'I never said that.'

'No, but it was pretty clear you meant it.'

'Honestly, I didn't.'

'No? What did you mean, then?'

He was deliberately baiting her now. There was a mocking lift to his voice which was unmistakable. But at least he wasn't angry. Perhaps if she tried again . . .

'*Would* you consider coming?' she asked hopefully, tightening her grip on the chairback and holding her breath.

'Maybe. If you ask nicely.'

'*Please*. I am asking nicely. We won't be able to make the trip without you.'

'That's better. Grovel some more.'

Damn him, thought Rosemary, not for the first time. But she had no choice. She grovelled. 'We really need you. Please. I'll be terribly grateful.'

'How grateful?' There was a speculative note in his voice now, along with the smug satisfaction which came with having the upper hand, and knowing it.

'Very grateful. I promise.'

'Hmm.' Jonathan pretended to give the matter deep consideration before replying in a lazily suggestive drawl, 'Well, in that case—I'll hold you to your promise, you know.'

Rosemary wished he was not fifteen miles away, because if he had been within throwing distance she would have taken great pleasure in hurling the nearest missile at his handsome, self-satisfied head. She glanced quickly around the kitchen. Yes. That egg-beater would have done nicely. He could do with egg on his face. She sighed.

Comforting as her daydreams were, they weren't going to help the current dilemma. So, instead of telling Jonathan that he couldn't hold her to any specific promise because she hadn't given him one, she made herself sound relieved—which she was—and appreciative, as she explained the arrangements for the trip, and said she would see him in the morning.

'Worse luck,' she muttered, as she quickly hung up the phone.

'But deep down she knew a jolt of excitement—and a sense of anticipation that she hadn't felt all week. Whatever else it might be, with Jonathan Riordan along, this was one field trip which would definitely not be dull.

By the time the Vancouver Island ferry pulled away from the dock at Horseshoe Bay the next morning, Rosemary was beginning to think that 'not dull' was a gross underestimation of reality. A nightmare seemed a more probable prognosis.

An assortment of parents delivered their charges to the dock on time, some anxious, and others obviously delighted to be disposing of their offspring for the weekend. That part went without a hitch. But the ferry was late, and when it finally arrived Tamsin and Debbie were nowhere to be seen.

'Oh, for God's sake. Can't you even control your own daughter?' snapped Rosemary, rounding on Jonathan. Her patience had worn thin during the delay, because Charlotte Little's mother had availed herself of the opportunity to pour a stream of contradictory instructions about the care and feeding of Charlotte into Rosemary's captive ear. And twenty minutes of Mrs Little was more than anyone should have to put up with on a wet Friday morning surrounded by restless, excited kids, thought Rosemary resentfully.

But Jonathan had been enduring a similar diatribe from a loud-mouthed father, and was in no mood to be snapped at by Rosemary—for whom, after all, he was taking a day off work at considerable inconvenience to himself. The extent of his altruism was only just beginning to dawn on him.

'I am not in charge of this trip, Miss Reid,' he replied grimly. 'My daughter is your responsibility as well as mine, you know.'

Henry Parkinson interrupted them hastily. 'Don't start bickering, you two. We haven't time for that now. Colin says Tamsin and Debbie are buying food at the restaurant over there.'

'Hell,' muttered Jonathan. 'I told her—oh, never mind; I'll fetch them. Get the rest of the gang on board.' With a parting glare at Rosemary, he strode off in the direction of the restaurant.

'Thanks a lot,' she grumbled, as she and Henry shouldered rucksacks and herded the students into their two cars ready to drive on board. 'You and I get thirteen kids between us, and his lordship Riordan gets two.'

'Only for a couple of minutes. And he *is* doing us a favour,' replied Henry reasonably. 'What is it with you two, anyway? I thought he was a friend of yours. Isn't that why you asked him?'

'I suppose it is. And you're right, of course. I was worried about Tamsin and Debbie, that's all. But he must have been just as anxious. Here they are now.'

Once on board, she sank back thankfully into an orange padded seat by the window as Jonathan loped towards them with Tamsin and Debbie in tow. Tamsin was looking sullen, Debbie scared—and Jonathan grim and scowling.

'You won't have any more trouble from these two for a while,' he assured her. 'That's right, isn't it?' He turned sternly to the two delinquents, who silently shook their heads.

'Well, I'm glad you're all here, anyway,' smiled Rosemary, in an effort to lighten the atmosphere. 'Tamsin and Debbie, why don't you go and join the others? Most of them are playing the videos, I think.'

'And the rest are probably falling overboard,' remarked Jonathan morosely. 'But perhaps that doesn't disturb you.'

'I wouldn't worry about them too much.' Henry beamed placatingly. 'They're sixteen years old, you know. And they're smart enough to join us before we get off the ferry.'

'I'm sorry I snapped at you, Jonathan.' Rosemary smiled up at him. He looked very forbidding, towering above her with his legs apart and the scowl firmly on his face. Oh, dear. They had three days to spend in each other's company, and those three days would be very uncomfortable if things were not put on a more amicable footing between them.

But now the scowl lightend perceptibly, and he lowered himself on to the seat beside her. 'You should be sorry,' he told her. 'I was beginning to think Tamsin was right when she called you the Dragon Lady.'

'Did she really?'

He smiled, a slow, sensuous smile that curled the tips of her toes. 'Mm. Not for a while, though. Do you really breath fire?'

From the smile playing on his lips, and the way his eyes were running over her body, Rosemary knew he was not talking about her temper, but about something else altogether. She bit the corner of her mouth and refused to meet his eyes.

'If you say so.'

Henry looked from Jonathan to Rosemary, and back again. 'I think I'll go check on the kids,' he murmured, rising quickly and bustling away before they could offer to go with him.

'Thoughtful of him,' remarked Jonathan. 'He's a nice fellow, isn't he? I can understand why you're such close friends.'

There was something in his voice that made Rosemary say quickly, 'Not that close,' and then wished she had kept her mouth shut when she saw that Jonathan was looking at her with that irritating gleam in his eyes. Why did he always know exactly what she was thinking, even when she hadn't said it?'

'No? I'm glad.' His arm was around her shoulders now, and she could feel the length of his thigh against her own. She gave a little shudder and he held her closer, gazing down at her with such an expression of sexy, tender affection that Rosemary felt her heart pounding against her rib-cage. Without quite meaning to, she leant her head on his shoulder.

Then she sat up quickly, remembering the lie he had spun her about his Saturday mornings.

'Tamsin says you don't even drink beer,' she said accusingly.

'I don't *what?*' choked Jonathan.

'Drink beer. On Saturdays. She said you go flying—or hang-gliding.'

'Ah. Traitorous child.' He grinned at her. 'But to my knowledge, neither of those activities appears in the cirminal code. So I don't see where there's a problem.'

Rosmary glared at him. 'You told me the Whiteheads made so much noise it always put you to sleep.'

'Did I? Well, they do, but in fact it has the effect of driving me out of the house.'

Rosemary glanced at him reprovingly and saw his grey eyes surveying her with amusement.

'You're an awful liar,' she told him reproachfully.

'I'm not. I'm a very good liar.'

Rosemary gave up, and put her head back on his shoulder.

'That's nothing to boast about,' she said severely. And then, after a while, 'Why do you go gliding? Isn't it dangerous?'

'It can be. But if you know what you're doing it's not hard to stay out of trouble. As for why . . .' He shrugged and didn't complete the sentence.

'I know,' said Rosemary drily. 'You do it because it's relaxing. All you have to do is strap yourself in a harness, jump off a cliff and float around in the updrafts.'

'How did you guess?' His arm was around her again, and Rosemary sat revelling in a sensation of warmth and closeness which she had not felt for many months. She was about to lift her hand to cover the one which was draped perilously close to her breast when she realised that two pairs of eyes were staring at them with voyeuristic glee.

She sat up hastily. 'Hi, Colin. Hi, Janey. Is there anything you need?' She tried to shrug off Jonathan's arm, but he only smiled blandly and moved his hand an inch away from temptation.

Colin and Janey shook their heads and continued to stare with wide, interested eyes.

'I think I'd better find Mr Parkinson,' said Rosemary, pushing Jonathan's arm away and jumping to her feet.

'Go ahead,' he agreed, grinning knowingly after her as his eyes followed her tall figure down the corridor. 'I'll stay with the baggage. I need the rest.'

Rest, snorted Rosemary to herself as she hurried past a group of pensioners on an outing. Flying, gliding, breaking up dog-fights. Rest, indeed. The man doesn't know what it means.

The remainder of the short journey to Vancouver Island passed, happily, without incident—apart from the inevitable discovery of Colin and Janey in a compromising embrace behind the video games. But that was so commonplace that it hardly qualified as an incident.

And those two had the nerve to stare at *me,* thought Rosemary crossly as she broke up the embrace with an efficiency born of long experience.

When the ferry neared Departure Bay, outside the Island town of Nanaimo, the three adults herded the students into their respective vehicles: Jonathan's Lincoln, Rosemary's Toyota and Henry's roomy station wagon. Colin and Kevin had brought their own cars, which helped to ease the congestion, but created another problem when Rosemary insisted that over her dead body was Janey Thatcher riding all the way to Pacific Rim National Park with Colin.

'Why can't I?' wailed Janey sulkily.

Rosemary did not feel like explaining that the facilities for sex-stops on the way to Long Beach—secluded picnic grounds, sandy lakesides beaches, and motels—might be too tempting to resist. Not that she had much faith that either Colin or Janey would even attempt to resist.

In the end Jonathan settled the situation by announcing in a firm, authoritative voice that there would be no more argument about it because Janey was travelling with him. Surprisingly, the opposition folded, and Janey, now looking more nervous than rebellious, climbed obediently into the Lincoln.

Two and a half hours later, after a drive that was interrupted only by a rest-stop by the towering Douglas Firs of Cathedral Grove and a brief pause to have a late lunch on the shores of Cameron Lake, the fleet of cars pulled up outside the office of the Porcupine Motel at Long Beach.

The misty rain which had shrouded their views on the way in cleared suddenly as they tumbled out of the cars on to the short expanse of grass which ran from the motel to the edge of the beach.

'We're here,' shouted a chorus of exultant young voices as they ran on to the sand to stare in awed delight down the miles of windswept beach. The gusty April wind shook the leaves of the trees, and in spite of all the evidences of civilisation, there was something vast and lonely and wild about the almost deserted beach with the breakers pounding ceaselessly against the sand and rocks and driftwood.

Rosemary took a deep breath of the clean, salt air, and felt Jonathan's fingers touch her arm softly through her white windbreaker.

'I'm glad you asked me to come,' he murmured, smiling down at her. The strong planes of his face were outlined against the sun and the breeze was blowing through his hair. He looked younger than Rosemary had every seen him.

'I'm glad, too,' she smiled.

'Come on, you two, let's get organised,' shouted Henry.

'Yes, no smooching in front of the class,' taunted Tamsin, as she hurtled past them with Charlotte and Colin in pursuit.

Jonathan extended a long arm and caught her by the scruff of the neck. 'And we don't need any cheek from you, young lady,' he told her sternly, as he pulled her round to face him.'

Tamsin squealed, but the lovely dark eyes in the solid little face sparkled up at Jonathan with tolerant affection

—and Rosemary knew suddenly that Tamsin didn't mind in the least that her once-despised teacher appeared to be getting on rather too well with her father.

That was certainly food for thought.

She had not wanted involvement with another man— not yet—but if it happened . . . Well, she was beginning to realise there was not much she could do about it. She was not yet ready to analyse too closely, but it was a fact that Jonathan Riordan had only to turn that slow, teasing grin on her and she melted immediately.

He was turning it on her now. She grinned back, and then the two of them walked side by side across the grass on the way to unload the cars.

Perhaps this weekend would not be such a disaster, after all.

They spent what was left of the day assigning cabins—Jonathan and Henry with nine boys between them in the first two, and Rosemary with the six girls in the third—storing rucksacks, unloading equipment, and generally getting organised for the fieldwork which would begin tomorrow. Rosemary and the girls cooked a substantial spaghetti dinner for the gang, and afterwards they all played cards for a while as Kevin strummed on a guitar. Eventually, as the exertions of the day began to take their toll, Rosemary suggested they should all get ready for bed.

It was after eleven when the lights were finally extinguished and, after much scuffling and giggling, everyone at last settled down for the night.

Thankfully, Rosemary closed her eyes.

Afterwards, she was never sure what it was that had disturbed her, but suddenly she was wide awake, with all her senses on edge. Something was wrong. She struggled up on one elbow and peered at the big double bed beside her. In the light from the moon which glinted through a chink in the curtains, she saw the shapes of two bodies breathing softly. In the sleeping-bag next to her own—there were not enough beds in the motel, and three of them had volunteered for the floor—another form lay outlined in the moonlight.

That left three to be accounted for. Rosemary slipped quietly out of her bag, shivering slightly in her thin cotton nightgown, and padded through the adjoining kitchen to the small extra room at the back.

As she pushed open the door, two more dark bodies stirred restlessly on the floor.

But the single bed against the wall was empty.

Rosemary closed her eyes, then opened them again. It didn't help. The bed was still empty. And the bathroom was dark and unoccupied.

She put out her hand to steady herself against the door.

It was Janey Thatcher, of course. It had to be. She might have known. Why *hadn't* she known? And what did she do now?

Very quietly she walked back to her own room and pulled the white windbreaker over her nightgown. Then she slid on socks and sneakers and stepped out into the night.

All right. Where was the obvious place to look? Where Colin Williams was, naturally. And where was Colin? In Jonathan's cabin, supposedly. But she was willing to bet he wasn't. All the same, that was the first place to check.

Catching her breath as the wind whistled over the beach and clamoured at her scanty clothing, Rosemary ran across to the cabin next door. She raised her arm to knock. But at the moment her hand should have made contact, the door flew suddenly wide and a large figure almost knocked her over as it hurled itself through the opening.

'Hell,' muttered a familiar voice, as the figure staggered against her, caught its footing, and put an arm around her waist to stop her falling.

Just for a moment their eyes held fast in the moonlight, and she felt Jonathan's arm tighten. Then almost in the same moment he let her go, and now she could see that his eyes were filled with the same concern as hers—an angry sort of concern, and for that she couldn't condemn him, because it was exactly the way she felt herself. If she could just get her hands on Janey . . . but of course that was the whole idea.

'Have *you* any idea where they might have got to?' asked Rosemary, not beating about the bush.

'No.' His tone was tight with a repressed emotion which boded no good for Janey and Colin—if they found them.

'What about Henry? What does he suggest?'

'Henry's asleep, I expect. No point in disturbing him. And I don't know what woke *me,* but something did.'

'I know. Me, too.'

There was a long silence, and Rosemary noted that his feet were bare beneath his jeans and that his belt was not done up. Her eyes moved upwards. A long-sleeved bush-shirt hung open over his waist, revealing the hard expanse of his chest. She gulped and raised her eyes higher. They were standing so close that she could see a muscle throbbing in his neck.

'On second thoughts, perhaps I do have an idea,' he said abruptly, turning his head towards the motel office. 'Come on.'

Fastening his belt with two quick movements, he grabbed her hand and began to pull her across the grass.

# CHAPTER EIGHT

'WHERE are we going?' gasped Rosemary, panting in the wake of this supposedly lethargic man who had turned suddenly into a human meteorite.

'Colin's car.' The words were tossed out of the side of his mouth and carried away on the wind.

'Where? Oh, Colin's car!' she exclaimed, as the white Cyclone Spoiler came into view, parked ostentatiously in front of the Porcupine's office. And then, 'Oh, dear.'

The Cyclone, which should have been a still, solid shape in the darkness, rocked slightly as if someone had lurched inside it. Jonathan broke into a sprint—but he was still gripping Rosemary's hand, and she slipped and stumbled behind him as he tore up to the unlocked door, heaved it open and bent down to glare inside. Rosemary, gasping, came to rest against the bonnet.

There was a sudden bone-chilling silence, then Rosemary heard Janey's voice raised in a pleading whine, 'Oh, please, Mr Riordan, it wasn't my idea—don't hit me, please.'

'Oh, lord,' groaned Rosemary, pulling herself upright and going to stand behind Jonathan. That's *all* I need. Newspaper headlines an inch thick announcing, 'Student Assaulted by Teacher on Island Field Trip.' Not that Jonathan was a teacher, but that was unlikely to deter the reporters. Well, perhaps it was no worse than 'Student Gets Pregnant on Trip Love-Trust.' She shuddered, and peered over Jonathan's shoulder.

He was reaching down to haul first Janey, and then Colin, on to the gravel parking-lot, where they crouched against the side of the car staring up at him with wide, frightened eyes. At least, Janey's eyes were frightened. Colin's seemed more indignant than scared. He was glaring at Janey as he mumbled sulkily, 'It was your idea.'

'It wasn't,' sniffed Janey. 'It was yours.'

Jonathan's fists, which were clenched tightly by the side of his thighs, loosened slightly and he took a step towards the troublesome couple.

'Shut up,' he snapped. 'Both of you. I don't care whose idea it was. And you can stop that snivelling, Janey. Much as I'd like to at the most, I have no intention of hitting you.'

Rosemary released her breath, and Jonathan rounded on her. 'For all they damn well deserve it,' he added. The grey eyes which were usually so calm and implacable smouldered angrily, and Rosemary drew in her breath again. God, he was marvellous when he looked like that. Like a medieval lord ruling his domain with the sublime arrogance of total authority and power.

She stared back at him, mesmerised, then, as he slowly turned away, she shook her head and came back to earth. This was no ancient fiefdom, but only a motel car park. And Jonathan was no lord, but only an angry man who had been worried to death by the antics of a couple of juvenile sex-fiends. And this field trip was *her* responsibility, not his. It was time she got things back on track.

'All right,' she said crisply to Colin and Janey. She pushed herself past Jonathan's broad back which was blocking her view of the two of them. 'Both of you. *Move*. Now. Back to bed—separately. I should send the pair of you straight home, but since that's quite impossible, I think we'd all better get some sleep—for what's left to us of the night. I'll talk to you both in the morning.'

The two miscreants nodded silently, straightened themselves, and sidled cautiously past Jonathan, who continued to glower at them threateningly.

As Rosemary and Jonathan followed them across the grass, they heard Colin say reproachfully to Janey, 'Why did you say it was my idea? You know you thought of it first.'

'Huh.' Janey tossed her head and they heard the words, 'Not much of a gentleman, are you?' float to them on the breeze.

'My God,' groaned Jonathan. 'After all the trouble those two have caused, disturbing my night and yours and landing themselves well and truly in the glue, all they can do is bicker about whose idea it was. How on earth do you stand it, Rosemary, week after week for years on end?' He smiled down at her with something which looked remarkably like admiration. Rosemary smiled back.

'I stand it because I love it. But don't ask me why. Maybe that's why I'm a teacher—and you're not.'

'Heaven forbid.' Jonathan rolled his eyes at the darkened treetops and squeezed her hand tightly. Her heart jumped, and she felt a familar curl of excitement in her stomach.

Fifteen minutes later all three cabins were quiet again. Nobody stirred, and Colin and Janey were both safely back in their beds.

Jonathan took a quick look around to make sure no one else was out of place, and stepped noiselessly outside. He glanced towards Rosemary's cabin and saw that she, too, was standing outside with her back against the door. Her hands were clasped behind her and her head was thrown back so that the delicate lines of her profile stood out clearly in the moonlight. The breeze was blowing her hair about her face, and Jonathan thought he had never seen anything so lovely at three o'clock in the morning on an early April night.

Softly he approached her across the grass, as the waves whispered over the sand and breakers foamed against the rocks.

As he came up to her, she turned her head. 'I thought you might come,' she said simply.

'Did you? I didn't know I was going to—but I must have known you were waiting.'

'Perhaps.'

'What were you waiting for, Rosemary?' His eyes on her face demanded an answer.

When it didn't come, he reached out his hand, turned her very gently towards him and pulled her into his arms. With a cry from the heart which only she could hear, Rosemary linked her hands behind his neck and raised her face to his.

Then she closed her eyes and held her breath.

His kiss seemed a very long time coming, and she could feel his warm breath on her cheek as she lifted her fingers to tangle them in his hair.

'Jonathan . . .' she whispered.

But her words were cut off, as with a small sound his lips closed over hers, and she felt his strong hands running down her spine. Then they circled her hips slowly and sensuously, and pulled her hard against him. Desire pounded through her body, as in some far-off world she heard the waves pounding on the beach. From his hair, she moved her fingers to his neck, then trailed them across his broad, bare chest. She felt the fine, smooth silkiness beneath her touch.

With another softer groan, Jonathan tore his lips from her mouth and began to kiss her eyelids, and her neck, and then his hand moved up to the V of her plain cotten nightgown—and suddenly, as she felt his touch against her breast, something stirred in her that was more than just passion. It was a feeling of tenderness and warmth, and a peace and sense of rightness she had never known before. She murmured softly against his chest, and then, as the sensation of happiness increased, the wind battered suddenly against the door, and she returned to a realisation of time and place—and saw that they were standing outside on a cold spring night, she in a windbreaker, nightgown and sneakers, he in an open shirt and bare feet—and with a cabin-load of sleeping children behind them.

Rosemary sighed and put both hands on the side of his head to push him reluctantly away.

'Rosemary, my love,' he protested, locking powerful arms around her waist and refusing to let her go.

Had he really called her his love? She shook her head, and the soft curtain of her hair fluttered against his face. His arms tightened convulsively.

'Jonathan, we mustn't,' she cried, struggling against his wonderfully hard male body and wishing only that she need not fight him—that she could sink blissfully into his embrace and lose the night to love.

'Why not?' His lips were against her ear and his

tongue flicked erotically around its rim.

'Because,' said Rosemary, bracing both palms against his bareness and giving an almighty shove, 'because, my single-minded, very sexy friend, we're responsible for those kids in there, and we've just given Colin and Janey hell for doing precisely the thing you want us to do. We're setting a terrible example. What if any of them wakes up?'

Unwilling, he released her. 'What if they do? I want you, Rosemary.'

Raising her eyes, from his heaving chest to the firm, virile mouth and the compelling grey eyes which seemed even deeper in the moonlight, Rosemary knew that she wanted him too, as she had never wanted anyone before. And not just for his body, either. She wanted all of him. She wanted the man who had laughed with her on the dyke and broken up a dog-fight, the man who had persuaded his partner to feign indigestion just so that he could see her again—and even the man who had come furiously, if misguidedly, to the defence of his difficult daughter—and then bought her a man-eating ferret to love because he couldn't give her a dog.

But this was not the place for wanting. Not here, where they were responsible for fifteen other-people's-children, and she was standing on the steps of a cabin on a beach listening to the wind and the waves—and wearing a windbreaker over a short cotton nightgown, and sneakers.

As she stared at the slightly belligerent angle of his chin, and the smoulder of thwarted passion in his eyes, Rosemary's mobile mouth curved suddenly into a totally unexpected smile. She hadn't known it was coming, but now she found herself trying not to laugh.

Her hilarity was caused partly by a glow of happiness because he wanted her, and partly by sheer amusement at the ridiculous picture they must present, or would present if anyone had been watching.

'What's so funny?' Jonathan's jaw jutted aggressively, and he scowled.

'Me,' she gurgled. 'Us. Here we are, making passionate love in the moonlight with the sound of the ocean in the background and the breeze blowing through our hair—and I'm wearing a windbreaker, sneakers and a nightgown.' She giggled again. 'It ruins the romantic image.'

Gradually Jonathan's rigid stance relaxed and his jaw lost its belligerence.

'Yes, I see your point,' he remarked in a strangled voice. And then, giving her a rakish grin, 'But I still think you're beautiful. And sneakers can always be removed—along with other things.

'No,' said Rosemary firmly. 'Not here they can't.'

'In the car, then.'

'Jonathan Riordan, I'm surprised at you.' Rosemary put her hands on her hips and tried to look severe, then remembered the sneakers and gave up. 'Just a little while ago you were mad as hell at the kids for turning their car into a love nest. Now you're suggesting we should do the same.'

Jonathan looked sheepish. 'It was just an idea,' he muttered. 'A temporary relapse to my teenage dating days. You're driving me crazy, you know, Rosemary Reid.'

'Am I? Serves you right. You've been driving me crazy ever since we met.'

'I'm glad.' He took a step towards her, but she

backed hastily away.

'No, Jonathan. Really. We have to go back inside. Besides . . .' She held out her hand. 'It's starting to rain—and there's work to be done in the morning. We'll both need our sleep if we're going to cope with the frightful fifteen tomorrow. You know very well we're in for a day of fun-filled chaos and mayhem.'

'That may very well be,' growled Jonathan with a shudder. 'But there's something I want a lot more than sleep.'

He looked so devastatingly attractive with his legs astride, head thrown back and the light of passion in his eyes, that Rosemary knew if she stood here with him for one moment longer she might not be responsible for her actions. Quickly, she held out her hand.

'No, please. Thanks for your help, Jonathan. Goodnight.'

Before he realised what she was about, she had pushed open the door behind her and darted back into the cabin.

He stared at the closed door, swore under his breath and slammed his fist into his palm. Then, with his jaw clenched tight he strode swiftly back to his cabin.

She was right, of course. This was not the time or place for what he had in mind. Not when they were in charge of fifteen teenagers whose hormones were active enough already without being encouraged by a demonstration from two people who were old enough to know better and supposed to be setting an example.

But he had not been joking when he'd told Rosemary she was driving him crazy. How he would get through another whole day without even touching her, he couldn't begin to imagine.

*        *        *

The tantalising aroma of pancakes and maple syrup wafted through the air to mingle with the damp, fresh smell of morning mist as Rosemary and her girls made their way over to Henry's cabin. The boys and Jonathan were there already, wolfing down pancakes like undernourished starlings.

In the ensuing commotion caused by the girls' conviction that the boys had eaten all the breakfast, Rosemary failed to notice that Jonathan had left the table and was nowhere to be seen.

As it turned out, there was plenty of food for everyone, and as soon as they had all finished she told her charges to collect their paraphernalia for the morning's expedition. But when she started to count noses she realised suddenly that four of the boys were missing.

'All right. Where are the rest of you?' she asked resignedly.

'Probably powdering their noses,' said Colin, unwisely drawing attention to himself.

Rosemary gave him a look of acute disfavour, and suggested that if he couldn't contribute anything useful to the conversation she'd be obliged if he would keep his brilliant wit to himself.

In the end it was Henry who told her, with his eyes fixed uncomfortably on his feet, that Jonathan had persuaded the four boys to go prospecting instead of spending the day investigating the tidal pools they had come so far to study.

'He what?' gasped Rosemary.

'He's going rock hunting or something. With some of the boys.' Henry cleared his throat, and his normally ruddy cheeks seemed more colourful than ever.

'But,' said Rosemary, ominously quiet now that she

knew the extent of Jonathan's perfidy, '*but*, this is suppose to be a *biology* trip. What have rocks got to do with it?'

'Don't know,' mumbled Henry. 'Better ask him.'

'You mean he's still here?'

'Think so. They went back to his cabin to pick up some food and a shovel.'

'I'll give him shovel,' fumed Rosemary, pushing past Henry and ignoring the eleven pairs of eyes relishing the prospect of trouble which followed her avidly through the door.

Her lips pressed angrily together, and her eyes flashing golden sparks, Rosemary crossed the grass to pound furiously on the door of Jonathan's cabin.

It opened immediately and there he stood, looking down at her with one hand raised casually above his head as he lounged against the doorframe.

'Good morning, Rosemary,' he drawled. 'And what can I do for you on this wonderful misty morning?'

'Oh!' exclaimed Rosemary, for a moment rendered speechless by his nonchalance. Didn't he even realise what he'd done? Or, at any rate was trying to do?

'Oh?'

The grey eyes regarded her with cheerful unconcern, and Rosemary took a firm grip on herself.

'Mr Riordan,' she began, as four tousled heads appeared from behind Jonathan's broad back and were waved peremptorily away, 'Mr Riordan, do you realise that this is supposed to be a biology field trip? Not an opportunity for you to use my students to drum up extra business for yourself.

He shruged, and the cheerful expression was replaced by a look of mild indifference.

'Yes, Rosemary, I do realise this is a biology trip. But education doesn't end with the set curriculum, you know, and as four of the boys expressed an interest in mineralogy, I saw no reason to discourage them.'

'You *wouldn't*,' replied Rosemary through clenched teeth. 'And I suppose in your view, just about everything is more important than the curriculum—concerts, sporting events, sunny days, visits to the dentist, visiting dignitaries, holidays in Hawaii—oh, and while we're at it, why aren't we teaching more physical education, more social skills, more health education, table manners, public-speaking and anti-littering? And then when all's said and done, and your child completes her schooling knowing how to add incorrectly, read badly, write illegibly, and nothing much else, you'll complain that your tax dollars are ill-spent on education. Well, guess what, Mr Riordan. I'm paid to teach these kids biology—and that's exactly what I intend to do. If you want to chase after mining prospects, you go right ahead. But you're doing it without my students.'

Jonathan's eyes ran thoughtfully over her body. Behind the cool grey veil of indifference, for a second Rosemary thought she detected a gleam of something which was almost—appreciation? Amusement? She closed her eyes, but when she opened them again the look was gone. She must have dreamed that she had actually ready sympathy in that quiet, impassive gaze.

Now he shifted his large body against the doorframe and put his hands in his pockets. 'Spoken with true conviction,' he said approvingly. 'But I'm not responsible for *all* the tribulations of your job, Rosemary. However, it's your decision. I'll tell the boys we'll have to postpone our expedition. Oh, and incidentally, the mining prospects in these parts are not inspiring, and I was *not* looking for business. There is a professor at the university who has a theory about deep-rooted plants picking up trace minerals which show in the leaves. As this whole area is rain forest, it seemed a good place to look for samples. I thought it might amuse the boys, that's all.'

'I see.' She was not mollified. 'Well, amusing the boys was not the purpose of the excursion, Mr Riordan.'

'Mr Riordan again? Are we back to that, Rosemary?'

He noticed that the freckles on her fair skin seemed to stand out more brightly when she was angry. And they made her more desirable then ever. He groaned inwardly because his ill-conceived plan to save his sanity by keeping out of the way of Rosemary the Untouchable for the day had only served to antagonise her. And she was right, as usual. He had had no business to sabotage her plans.

He looked at her now, standing with her ballet-dancer's feet turned slightly outwards, and her willowy body swaying enticingly towards him. Then he saw her eyes, and knew that enticement was the last thing she had on her mind.

'All right,' he said quietly. 'I'll explain to the boys. And of course I'll stay to help you. After all, that's why I came.'

'I'm glad you've remembered that,' said Rosemary acidly. 'But there's no need to if you'd rather not. We can manage without you, you know.

'Yes, so you have frequently reminded me. All the same, I'll be there.'

'Right.' Rosemary turned quickly on her heel and

walked away from him with her nose held haughtily in the air.

Damn him, anyway. Last night he had been warm and gentle and had wanted to make love to her. But in the cold light of morning he had apparently become his old arrogant self again, and decided with selfish unconcern to arrange her field trip entirely to suit himself.

She should never have asked him to come.

Behind her, Jonathan watched her go, and slammed his hand frustratedly against the doorpost. This was ridiculous. He didn't need Rosemary as a permanent blot on his landscape any more than she needed him. So why was he angry with her for saying she could manage without him? She had better manage without him, because the last time a woman had relied on him for support, he had let her down badly—so badly that she had died.

For the remainder of a very active day, during which the normal West Coast rain stayed miraculously away, and the sun appeared intermittently through the mist, Rosemary, Jonathan and Henry supervised the collection of a fascinating assortment of sea-life: sculpins, starfish, crabs, sand dollars, and even a small octopus which was kept in large pail—until he started to turn a peculiar greyish-green.

'We'd better put him back in the sea,' said Rosemary quickly.

'I'll do it.'

Before anyone could move, Kevin jumped up and was running across the rocks with the pail swinging from his hand. A moment later the octopus was back in the ocean—and Kevin was poised perilously on the side of a steep, weed-slicked rock as he swung round to return to his classmates.

With a muttered oath, Jonathan hurled himself to his feet and leaped towards the dangerously teetering figure. Henry and Rosemary were left gaping in the rear as he grabbed Kevin around the waist with one arm and jerked him back from the edge. For a moment their bodies swayed above the frothing grey waves, then Rosemary's heart returned to its rightful place, as Jonathan caught his balance and led a white-faced Kevin back to his gasping friends.

Once again she was struck by the speed at which this proponent of ease and relaxation seemed to move as a matter of course.

She gave him a grateful smile.

'Truce?' he asked, raising his dark eyebrows irresistibly.

'Truce,' agreed Rosemary with resignation.

As the day at long last drew to a close, and they began to pack up their belongings, Jonathan stood alone on the shore for a few quiet seconds, and watched Rosemary at work—collecting, explaining, answering questions, and still managing to remain calm and smiling. For the first time he understand just how how wrong he had been when he had burst into her classroom like an irate bull in a children's zoo and accused her of being incompetent.

Then she jumped and brushed a passing fly from her nose, and he saw that she was no longer looking at the collected specimens in the pool, but staring upwards at the grey-flecked sky.

'Look,' she said, pointing.

High above them a bald eagle circled and flew lower—then lower still. For a moment it perched at the very top of a dark green pine tree, and then, as they stared in absorbed fascination, it circled again and dived. A small, black-headed scoter, lagging behind its companions, dipped quickly beneath the waves. But when it came up again, the eagle struck, and the little duck was no more.

'Fascinating,' breathed Rosemary. 'I've never seen that before.'

'Ugh!' cried Charlotte with a shudder. 'That was gross.'

It was obvious that she was not the only one who was more horrified than fascinated. Biology was one thing. Nature in the raw quite another. So Rosemary was glad that on their way back to the cabins that evening they passed an offshore islet, and there on the sea-scarred rocks lay a colony of steller sea-lions. One huge bull, who looked as though he could easily weigh two thousand pounds, lifted his head as they passed in the distance, and barked accusingly. A cacophony of sound broke out as the others followed his lead.

'Trespassers please leave name of next-of-kin,' murmured Jonathan.

Everyone laughed, and a short time later, tired and conscious of a job well done, the small party returned thankfully to their cabins.

When, after an hour had passed, and no interesting aroma of food was drifting over to tempt their taste-buds, Rosemary, Tamsin and another girl walked over to Henry's cabin to investigate.

They found most of the boys, plus four girls, happily playing poker. Henry and Jonathan were sprawled idly on the only two easy chairs, their eyes half-heartedly scanning pieces of yesterday's paper.

'Huh,' snorted Rosemary. 'Just as I thought. Come on, you lot. Your turn to make supper.'

Henry raised his eyes and gave her his best engaging grin. 'But we already made breakfast,' he protested.

'Won't wash,' commented Jonathan, shaking his fair head and drawing up long legs to rise reluctantly to his feet. 'The sergeant major here wants us to cook supper.' His grey eyes issued a challenge. 'On the other hand, she can make breakfast tomorrow.'

'Of course,' said Rosemary, tilting her nose at him and trying to look offended. 'Fair's fair—and I'm not a sergeant major.'

'You could have fooled me,' murmured Jonathan, giving her a lopsided grin that made her heart turn over. 'How about a slave-driver, then?'

'How about a ravenously hungry lady who is about to attack the chefs if they don't produce food in very short order?'

'Hmm,' said Jonathan, his eyes running suggestively over her body. 'I could live with that. How about you, Henry?'

'With a meat tenderiser,' added Rosemary threateningly.

'All right, all right.' Jonathan held up his hands in surrender and ambled over to the stove. 'Come on, Henry. The sergeant has spoken.'

Henry put aside his paper, lifted his shoulders in an embarrassed little shrug, and joined Jonathan at the stove.

Rosemary watched the two of them put together meat, beans and tomatoes to whip up a very passable chilli, and decided she felt quite charitable towards Jonathan again. Her anger of the morning had dissipated entirely when he'd rescued Kevin from the rocks. What was more, Henry could take a few lessons from him on how to get on with the job. Comfortable Henry, who lived with his mother, was so busy trying to organise the boys into helping that he was accomplishing very little himself.

Her eyes strayed back to Jonathan, who with his sleeves rolled back was competently stirring the pot, and she thought for the hundredth time what a contradictory man he was. Sometimes warm and tender and utterly irresistible. But often, too often, there was something hard and impregnable about him—like a tough granite wall. Glancing at his daughter now, she wondered if the roots of the hardness lay in his marriage to Tamsin's mother. Then she smiled disparagingly at herself.

Whatever it was that made Jonathan the man he was, it could make no possible difference to her.

After supper, they all played cards. Rosemary sat next to Jonathan, and Tamsin laughed when her teacher succeeded in gaining control of the hearts' game three times out of five, to make Jonathan a very solid loser.

'You're not used to losing hearts, are you, Dad?' chuckled Tamsin, giving her father an affectionate poke in the ribs.

The girl had blossomed on this trip, thought Rosemary. After the bad start when she and Debbie had almost missed the ferry, Jonathan's child had been a model student—cheerful, helpful and a pleasure to be with.

But Jonathan was not looking at his daughter now. Instead he had turned towards Rosemary, so that his elbow brushed her arm.

'I'm not so sure,' he replied, staring into her eyes with surprise, dawning comprehension—and very little pleasure. 'I'm not sure about that at all.'

With an effort, Rosemary tore her eyes away. She saw Tamsin was glancing between the two of them with a funny, perceptive smile on her small mouth.

And she doesn't mind, thought Rosemary with a start. My Impossible Student of the Year really wants her father to like me.

That brought her up short. Because liking was one thing—but she was no more used to losing hearts than Jonathan was. And at the back of her mind was the devastating notion that, if she let herself lose it this time, she might never get it back.

Then suddenly Jonathan was standing up. 'If nobody minds, I'm going for a walk,' he said abruptly. He made for the door with a restless, very physical energy she had often observed in him before.

'Want some company?' asked Henry. 'The game's over now and I could use the exercise. You can manage these hellions for a while, can't you, Miss Reid?'

Rosemary looked dubious, but several of the hellions grinned and said they were tired anyway, so she nodded and said that if everyone was going to bed there shouldn't be any problem. As Colin and Janey appeared not to be speaking today, she anticipated no problem from that quarter, either.

Jonathan looked suddenly broody and intense, unlike the man who a few moments earlier had been lounging over the table casually dealing cards. And Rosemary did not believe he wanted company in the least.

But a minute later the two men vanished into the night.

Rosemary settled the girls down quickly and said she would be back as soon as she had checked that all was well with the boys.

She knocked quietly on the door of Henry's cabin. A chorus of sleepy voices assured her that everything was fine. She received the same answer from Jonathan's group.

The ocean was hissing darkly across the sand, ink-black and mysterious under the pale white moon.

On an impulse, Rosemary strolled down to the beach. She watched the waves frothing at her feet, and then raised her head to stare out into the blackness of the Pacific. Her mind had gone strangely blank now that she was alone, away from clamouring students and with only the wind and the sea to break the eerie silence of the night.

A man coughed somewhere in the distance, and she was reminded of where she was, and that she was supposed to be watching over three cabin-loads of creative adolescents.

With one last glance at the ocean, she hurried back to her charges.

Everything was quiet, and it was only as she was about to pull off her bulky sweater that she sensed that, once again, something was not right. No, she thought, closing her eyes. It couldn't be. Not two nights in a row. But she was still had an odd sensation that something was out of place. Was that *whispering* she heard outside the door? She crossed to the back room. Janey was peacefully in her bed. But the lump on the floor that was supposed to be Tamsin was only a rumpled khaki sleeping-bag.

'Damn,' said Rosemary, so loudly that the two sleeping bodies shifted positions and muttered indignantly. 'Damn.' And damn Henry and Jonathan, too. If they had just stayed put, she need never have left the cabin.

The whispering outside became louder, and Rosemary opened the door again to slip quietly into the night.

There was no one in sight, and the sounds seemed to be coming from round the back. She moved swiftly in the direction of the voices.

Two figures were crouched on the ground, their bodies huddled against the wall. One was Tamsin. The other was Colin Williams, and his arm was around Tamsin's shoulders. Her face was twisted towards him and his forehead was resting lightly against her hair.

'Tamsin!' began Rosemary in an agonised hiss. But, just as she moved to separate the love-birds another figure erupted round the opposite corner, and with a muffled but very explicit curse swept down on the two on the ground, seized Colin by the shoulder and practically flung him against the wall. With his other hand he grabbed the back of Tamsin's jacket and hauled her to her feet.

Rosemary's hand flew to her mouth as she saw that Jonathan was not looking at Tamsin. Instead his eyes were fastened on his daughter's teacher, and the expression in their seething grey depths was as explosive as she had ever seen it—and filled with furious accusation.

# CHAPTER NINE

'So this is your idea of supervision, Miss Reid. I can't say I'm impressed.' Jonathan's words were bitten short, and his voice rigidly controlled, but Rosemary had the impression that it was only with greatest difficulty that he prevented himself from reaching out to strike her.

'It's not Miss Reid's fault,' Tamsin interrupted bravely, her big, dark eyes fixed anxiously on her father.

'If I want your opinion, I'll ask for it,' he snapped. 'Colin, I'll talk to you—again—later. Tamsin, I'll talk to you in a minute. Go back inside and wait for me. Right now, I want a word with Miss Reid.'

'Here?' asked Rosemary, in a voice which came out irritatingly like a squeak.

'It's as good a place as any. As my daughter and young Colin appear to have discovered.'

'I don't think they were doing anything very drastic,' said Rosemary slowly, as Colin and Tamsin slunk off in separate directions.

'Oh, don't you? Sometimes, Rosemary, I wonder if you think at all. Don't you realise you were in charge of those children? Yet you couldn't even keep track of them for fifteen minutes. As far as I know, Group Groping and High Tech Sex are *not* part of Mathieson High's curriculum.' He took a step towards her and rested his hand dangerously close to her ear as she pressed back against the wall of the cabin. 'If I hadn't appeared on the scene,' he went on, 'my sixteen-year-old daughter . . .'

Not for the first time since she had known Jonathan Riordan, Rosemary's temper flamed sky-high. She had had an exhausting day, her emotions had been on edge for weeks, and now this impossible, unreasonable man who seemed to have such a devastating effect on her was accusing *her* of irresponsibility. After *he* had wandered off for a stroll, leaving her to keep a mere two eyes on fifteen boisterous, resourceful teenagers.

'*Mr* Riordan,' she interrupted hotly, ducking quickly under his arm. 'Mr Riordan, if you hadn't appeared on the scene, your sixteen-year-old daughter would be exactly where she is now. Safely in her cabin. I was away for about ten minutes—among other things checking on the boys who were supposed to be *your* responsibility. And Colin and Tamsin must have had all of five minutes together. From what I could see, all they were doing was talking. If you were a half-decent father to that child, she might talk to you instead of sneaking off behind your back. Buying her clothes and the odd carnivorous ferret is *not* all that fatherhood involves.'

She had drawn herself up to her full height as she spoke, but Jonathan's body loomed larger in the moonlight and Rosemary saw him ram his hands forcefully into his pockets. His lips, which she knew could be warm and caressing, were stretched in a tight, bitter line. But something in his frozen stance caused her to look at him more closely, and just for a moment she thought she saw, not anger, but a bleak despair in his eyes.

Then he rested a shoulder against the wall and his mouth twisted contemptuously.

'Of course, you have such wide experience of parenthood, *Miss* Reid. Naturally that makes you an expert.'

Rosemary opened her mouth, closed it again, and drew her windbreaker closer around her body.

'I may not be an expert on parenthood,' she said, quietly now, 'but I do know something about kids. I've been teaching them for six years. And I can tell you one thing. Tamsin thinks the world of you, but she's not at all sure what you think of her. I don't know why, but she's been much happier these last few weeks. Don't blow it now by handling tonight like Attila the Hun on a parental rampage. And please don't blame your deficiencies as a parent on me. I'm very fond of Tamsin, but you're the only one who can make something good come out of this mess—instead of turning it into a complete castastrophe.'

She had been looking at the ground while she spoke, unable to bear the scorn in his eyes, and when she finished speaking she started to turn away from him. But his arm flashed out and spun her around to face him. A moment later she felt his hand beneath her chin as he pushed her head upwards.

There was no contempt in his eyes now. Only a kind of hard, deliberate searching. His fingers tightened on her chin and his fair head started to bend towards her. Then, with a small, exasperated exclamation, he dropped his hand, gave her an intent yet oddly baffled glare, and, turning on his heel, vanished swiftly around the corner.

Rosemary stared at the place where he had disappeared. Then, giving herself an abrupt shake, she made her way quickly to the front of the cabin.

When she reached the door again, she saw him walking towards the ocean with Tamsin, who must have been watching out for him. Rosemary thought he looked like some pagan god of old, silhouetted black and massive against the moon, with the small, sturdy acolyte trotting obediently beside him.

Well, he was not any god *she* wanted to worship, she told herself furiously, as the two figures faded into the darkness. She wished she had not been forced to ask Jonathan on this trip. It had been an unmitigated disaster from the beginning. Well—perhaps not quite unmitigated. She remembered the feel of his arms around her last night, the touch of his hands on her hair and the warm male scent of his body. He had called her 'my love' and for a very brief space she had known a happiness and closeness that she had never experienced before.

But, as she snuggled down inside her sleeping-bag a few minutes later, she kept seeing Jonathan's angry, accusing eyes as he glared at her in the moonlight over Tamsin's startled head. And she could understand his anger. Fathers were not noted for sweet reason when it came to the welfare of their beloved only daughters. And, in spite of what she had said in the heat of the moment, she knew that he cared deeply for Tamsin—it was one of the things she liked about him—and that he did try his best to be a good father.

From that conclusion, her thoughts strayed one step further. Of course, it was obvious. What Tamsin really needed was a mother.

And then, with a terrifying sense that the cabin was falling down about her ears, it came to her. If Tamsin needed a mother, she, Rosemary, wanted to be that mother. She wanted to look after Tamsin, to help her grow into the bright, intelligent young woman she would some day become. And, yes, she wanted everything else that that implied. She wanted Jonathan Riordan—not just for now, but for always.

She gave a little groan of dismay. She might have known it. She had been fooling herself when she'd insisted that after Ronald her heart would remain free and independent. Independent, maybe. But free? No. It would never be free again.

At that point in her thoughts, Rosemary stopped short. Even if Jonathan were not blazing angry with her, he would never ask her to marry him. He had told her that he had tried marriage once and that it was an experiment he was not anxious to repeat. Oh, he wanted her, of course. There was no question about that.

But wanting had nothing to do with marrying.

For a long time she lay staring into the darkness—remembering. Jonathan teasing her about grey hair, pursuing the dogs on the dyke, joking with his daughter—and the bleakness in his eyes when he mentioned his wife. And then, in the end, his tall figure walking away from her in the moonlight.

She sighed, and to her surprise found herself stifling a yawn. Of course, it *had* been a very tiring day, and now it was very late. Perhaps things would be clearer in the morning . . .

Her eyelids drooped, and a few minutes later she was asleep.

Rosemary was right. In the morning, things were indeed clearer. All too hopelessly clear.

As she was heaving her pack towards the car park, Jonathan came up beside her, took it from her and slung it over his shoulder.

'I apologise for my tirade of last night,' he said quietly. 'Of course we should never have left you to cope with the children on your own.'

'I don't see why not,' said Rosemary shortly. 'You had no way of knowing what would happen. And anyway, nothing did happen.'

'I know. I've spoken to Tamsin.'

His voice was curt, taut with control, and Rosemary did not envy Tamsin what must have been a very unpleasant interview.

They had reached the car park now, and Jonathan lowered her pack to the ground beside the Toyota. He was staring above her head towards the sea, and the look in his eyes was dark now and altogether empty. 'I also apologise for what happened on Friday night.'

Rosemary stared up at him, stunned and puzzled by the coldness on his face. 'You don't have to aplogise for that,' she said quietly.

'I do, I'm afraid.' He was still not looking at her. 'It wasn't fair to you.'

'I don't see why not,' replied Rosemary drily, feeling the stirrings of a familiar annoyance. 'I've yet to fall apart because of a kiss. And in case you happen to have forgotten, that's all it ever was.'

'I haven't forgotten.'

'Then what's the big drama, Jonathan? Afraid you're committed for life?'

Oh, God, what had made her say that to him? That wasn't what she wanted to say at all.

But Jonathan's hands were on her shoulders, and the grey eyes staring into hers were filled with a hard authority.

'Cut it out, Rosemary. Sarcasm doesn't become you. I'm trying to set the record straight, that's all.'

'What record? I didn't know there was one.' Somehow she couldn't stop her tongue.

Jonathan's strong jaw became more pronounced, and the lines around his eyes deepened. In the distance the clamour of voices grew louder as someone shouted that they ought to leave in a minute.

'I'm telling you, Rosemary, cut it out and listen. I've enjoyed being with you. And I admit my original idea was to . . .'

'Get me into bed?' Her head was tilted defiantly, and there were two spots of crimson on her cheeks.

Jonathan drew in his breath. 'Right. You've got it,' he said harshly.

'And now you've changed your mind?'

His fingers were digging into her shoulders now, and the voices were coming very close. 'No,' he said bitingly, 'I have *not* changed my mind. I find it very hard to keep my hands off you, Rosemary. Sometimes in more ways than one. Which is why I wanted to spend yesterday with as many miles as possible between us. But——' he moved his hands abruptly and gave her a steely, tight-lipped smile '—but I'm glad you had the sense to stop me the other night, because there's no future for us now, nor will there ever be. And I've no right to use you when I can't give you anything in return.'

The hard knot in Rosemary's stomach burst suddenly, and she bent to pick up her pack so that he couldn't see the tears in her eyes.

'You needn't worry,' she told him over her shoulder. 'Because you don't have anything to give me that I want.'

She was fumbling, misty-eyed, with the clasp on her rucksack, so she didn't see the pain which momentarily darkened his eyes. Then a party of yelling teenagers cannoned into him, and he was drawn laughingly off to help them load the cars.

A feeling of utter desolation engulfed Rosemary. She straightened slowly, and it was as if an iron fist were squeezing the life from her heart.

And it wasn't true. He had the only thing she had ever wanted him to give. Himself.

With a silent, inward cry, she seized the rucksack and hurled it violently into the boot. In keeping with her mood, it had started to rain again.

They were already nearing Port Alberni before she realised that the two girls occupying the back seat were sleeping, and that the quiet, solid little body sitting beside her was Tamsin. The girl's eyes were fixed worriedly on her teacher's face, and she seemed to be waiting to speak.

Rosemary made a effort to smile. 'Sorry, Tamsin,' she murmured, 'I was so lost in my thoughts that I hardly knew you were there. How come you're not with your father?'

'Because I wanted to ride with you.'

'I see. And I should at least have known you were here, shouldn't I?'

Tamsin shook her head. 'It's all right. I've been watching you. It's my father, isn't it? You looked like I often used to feel.'

Rosemary eyed her curiously. 'What do you mean?'

'Well, ever since Mother died, Dad's always been nice to me—but sometimes I felt he wasn't really there, wasn't listening—as though he was trying to do what fathers are expected to do, but—didn't really know what that was—and, well you know—didn't much care. And when he got like that it made me feel awful. That's what you looked like just now. As if he'd made you feel awful.'

Rosemary smiled at the square little face gazing so earnestly into hers. 'Did I? And I suppose that's why you were particularly awful at school. You decided you didn't care, either.'

Tamsin turned her head away. 'Yes. Only you wouldn't let me not care.'

'No, I wouldn't, would I? And then you got angry and behaved even worse. Because you were angry already, and it was easier to be angry with me than with your father.'

Tamsin ran her finger around the 'thank you for not smoking' sign on the dashboard. 'Mm,' she mumbled. 'But I'm not angry any more. Dad's been different lately. He's always been sort of easy-going, but for the last few weeks he's actually seemed, well, happy—sometimes.'

'Wasn't he happy before?'

'I think so, but he was never around much before Mother died, so I don't know what he was like then.'

'He must miss her very much.' Rosemary felt the fist tighten further around her heart. 'You both must.'

But Tamsin was shaking her head.

'I did, of course, especially at first. But I don't think Dad does, really. He never saw much of her, anyway. I think he just feels guilty.'

Rosemary stared at her, startled out of her own misery. 'Guilty? That's an odd thing to say. Why should he feel guilty?'

'I don't know,' replied Tamsin. And then, with a finality that brooked no argument, 'But he *does*.'

'Oh.' Rosemary looked at the car ahead where Jonathan's fair head was visible through the window. Then it occurred to her that her preoccupation with the father was making her forget the needs of the daughter. She ought to talk to her about last night, and the moonlight tryst with Colin behind the cabin. But she found she didn't want to speak of it at all. The memory of last night was too painful.

'You're happier now, aren't you, Tamsin?' she asked, putting off the evil moment. 'I've enjoyed having you in my class lately.'

The girl nodded shyly. 'Yes. I like being there, too. But I think Dad's gone all private again.'

'Has he?' Rosemary felt a lump growing in the back of her throat. She swallowed, but it wouldn't go away.

'Mm. Miss Reid . . .?'

'Yes?'

'I wondered . . . I thought for a while . . . I mean . . .'

'What did you wonder, Tamsin?'

'I wondered if you and Dad might be going to—well, you know, get married. I kind of hoped you would.' The last words came out in a breathless rush, and Rosemary was more touched by the girl's admission than she would have believed possible a few weeks ago.

She shook her head regretfully. 'No,' she said, unaware of the sadness in her voice. 'No. I like your father very much, Tamsin. But we really don't know each other very well—and we won't be getting married. Why do you want us to?'

Tamsin's big eyes studied her face. 'Because—because lately I've been realising I was wrong. Dad does care about me . . .'

'Of course he does. I expect you're just seeing things more clearly now because you're growing up.

Tamsin nodded. 'Yes, maybe. Anyway, although Dad never says so, I can tell he's lonely sometimes. I don't think he really talks to his gold-diggers . . .' She paused, and a bright blush covered her cheeks. 'Oh, dear, I didn't mean . . .'

For the first time that day Rosemary found herself

smiling. 'I know what you mean. And I'll *bet* he doesn't do much talking.'

Tamsin grinned and the flush faded quickly. 'He says he likes his life the way it is. And I suppose he does, in a way. But next year I'll be off to university. I hope go get into McGill, and that's thousands of miles away.'

'Yes, I see. And you know your father will miss you.' She hesitated. 'All the same, you're an unusual young woman, Tamsin. Most sixteen-year-olds who have had their fathers to themselves for some time aren't any too anxious to share them with anyone else. Even for a short time.' She smiled wryly. 'And especially not when that someone else is a teacher they used to hate.'

'I didn't hate you. I knew that as soon as Dad told me I had to leave your class.' Suddenly Tamsin's brown eyes lit up with an imp of mischief. 'And besides—if you could meet some of Dad's gold-diggers, you'd see why I'd rather have you.'

'Thanks. I'm just as glad I haven't met them.'

'Yes, you're lucky. Deloraine's the worst.'

Rosemary decided that discussing Jonathan's mistresses with his daughter would hardly pass the standards of professional conduct laid down in the Code of Ethics. She swung round a bend in the dark, tree-lined road and changed the subject quickly. 'Mrs Peacock, though. You do like her, don't you?'

'Oh, Mrs Peacock.' Tamsin shrugged. 'She keeps the house all right. But she won't look after Dracula.'

'She won't?'

'Nope. Mrs Whitehead next door is feeding her this weekend.'

'That's nice of Mrs Whitehead,' said Rosemary, uncharitably wondering if Tamsin's sudden enthusiasm for a stepmother had anything to do with the care and feeding of ferrets. Then she decided she was being unfair—and remembered that, in any case, if the question of Jonathan's remarriage was academic, the subject of Tamsin's behaviour last night most certainly was not. Quietly, and without accusation, she asked Tamsin what had happened between her and Colin.

Tamsin twisted the ends of her hair nervously. 'It wasn't what you think,' she replied, after a short silence.

'What was it, then?'

'Well, you see, Colin and Janey had a fight. And Colin asked me if I'd meet him privately—so he could talk to me about Janey. She's a friend of mine, and he thought I might know what he ought to do.'

'Hm,' said Rosemary sceptically. 'But that doesn't explain why he had his arm around you, Tamsin. And in any case, you knew very well you had no business to be out of your bed.'

'I know. But I wanted to help. And I didn't think it could hurt anyone. And his arm didn't mean anything. Colin's just a touching sort of person.'

'I don't doubt it,' replied Rosemary drily. 'Have you explained all that to your father?'

'Yes. But I think he's still mad at me. Is he still mad at you, Miss Reid?'

'I'm afraid he may be.'

'Oh, dear. And it's all my fault. And I only wanted to help.'

Tamsin looked so woebegone that Rosemary was sorry for her. It took the remainder of the drive to Departure Bay to convince the girl that Jonathan's feelings about Rosemary had nothing to do with his daughter, and that nobody's life had been irrevocably ruined by her thoughtlessness.

Although, when she thought about it, Rosemary was not at all sure that the latter assertion was true.

Once on board the ferry, most of the now somewhat weary little group headed for the cafeteria with single-minded unity.

'They've been suffering from hamburger withdrawal,' remarked Henry, grinning. 'They're all in need of a fix.'

'I know.' Rosemary, who had lost interest in food, opened a thermos and poured herself some coffee. 'Aren't you joining them? Where's Jonathan?'

'Last seen making for the video games. With a very dour look on his face.'

'The video games?' Rosemary gaped at him. 'Isn't he a little old for that?'

Henry shrugged, his round blue eyes puckering at the corners. 'Why don't you ask him? I suppose there's a little of the kid in all of us.'

But when Rosemary did eventually wander in the direction of the games, she saw that there was nothing remotely childlike about the way Jonathan was manipulating the handle of the nearest blinking electronic marvel. He was gripping it as though he would subdue the world with its aid, and the little moon-shaped mouth on the screen was gobbling up dots with a manic, frenzied urgency. Jonathan's own mouth was clamped tightly shut. His jaw was hard and his arm propelled the handle with the set, automatic movements of a machine. Behind him, several wide-eyed youngers were watching his grim-faced prowess with awed admiration.

Rosemary took a step forwards him, then changed her mind. Just at the moment, she decided, it might be unwise to get too near that ruthless, forcing arm.

When they finally left the ferry, and the children were picked up by smiling anxious parents—and a few who looked as if they could have supported the absence of their offspring for a much longer period—Henry asked Rosemary if she was all right.

'Of course,' she replied, surprised.

'Oh. Good. It's just that—Riordan . . .' His words trailed off and he stared uncomfortably at the ground.

Rosemary looked back at the ferry terminal. Jonathan was just drawing away from the kerb, and a moment later the Lincoln pulled up beside them.

She caught a glimpse of Tamsin's white face in the passenger seat as Jonathan leaned through the window and said tersely, 'Thanks for a memorable weekend.' There was no warmth in his voice, and his eyes were cold and strained.

'That's all right. Thank you for coming.' Her reply was polite and very cool, but she was forced to keep a tight rein on her tongue to prevent herself from screaming.

Jonathan nodded, his expression unchanged. Only Tamsin looked stricken.

With a hasty, almost guilty goodbye to the girl and her father, Rosemary climbled into the Toyota.

Five days later, she climbed into Henry's station wagon. Her own car was once more in for repairs, and Henry, with his usual good nature, had offered to take her home from school.

'You've been looking peaky this week, Rosemary Reid,' he remarked quitely, as they crossed the bridge into Richmond. 'Was that wild weekend at Long Beach too much for you?'

Rosemary smiled. No, of course not. Well . . . yes, in

one way I suppose it was.' She hadn't meant to say that, but there was something very comforting about Henry's friendly concern, and she felt a sudden need for comfort.

And it seemed Henry understood. 'Riordan?' he asked, his ginger-coloured eyebrows disappearing into his hair.

Rosemary stared through the window. They were passing a garden full of Japanese plum trees in full blossom. Somehow the sight of their bright pink promise, combined with Henry's caring, made her feel peakier than ever.

'I suppose so,' she admitted slowly. And then more definitely, and with a determined lifting of her chin, 'But of course it's very silly of me.'

'What is?'

'Letting Jonathan's behaviour last weekend upset me. I mean—he doesn't *mean* anything to me.'

'Doesn't he?' Henry's eyes were on the road.

'No. Not really. I only asked him to come because there was no one else.'

Liar, she thought. Who did she think she was fooling?

A whole week had passed since she had seen Jonathan. A week during which he had made no attempt to contact her. And she had discovered that she missed him terribly—that it looked as though for her there would never by anyone else. And because she could not have him, that meant she would always be alone.

She sighed, and Henry looked at her sharply. 'Perhaps he's out of town,' he suggested. 'Have you asked Tamsin?'

'No, but she told me. He's in Vancouver all right, and acting like Eeyore with the migraine one moment, and wolfman on the prowl the next. His daughter says the procession of gold-diggers goes up and down in direct proportion to which animal he's impersonating.'

'Animal? Gold-diggers?'

'The donkey or the wolf. And gold-diggers are what Tamsin calls his ladyfriends.'

Henry snorted. 'Respectful little brat, isn't she?'

Rosemary laughed. Talking to Henry always made her feel better. And Tamsin's description of Jonathan was probably all too accurate. 'I don't know about respectful, but she had a very perceptive eye where her father is concerned.'

'Humph,' grunted Henry gloomily. 'I wish it was equally perceptive where mathematics was concerned. Never mind. You're laughing again. Want to go out tomorrow night?'

'With you?'

'Well—for lack of any ne better.' He smiled at her, a gentle, self-deprecating smile.

'Oh, Henry! I didn't mean that, you know I didn't. It's just . . .' She hesitated, fumbled for words. 'I'd love to go out with you. It's just that I wouldn't want you to think that I—well, that I wanted to get serious, or—or married—or anything like that.'

They were pulling into her driveway now, and Murphy was barking at the strange car moving into his territory. When she turned to look at Henry, she saw that he was staring at her with an expression of advanced horror on his ruddy face.

'Good God!' he exclaimed, in a scandalised voice. 'Whatever gave you that idea? Why on earth should I want to get serious or——' he shuddered '—married? I'm entirely comfortable as I am, and I never thought you . . .'

He was as close to apoplexy as Rosemary had ever seen him, and she burst out laughing.

'Oh, Henry, what a tonic you are, ' she gasped, tears of laughter running down her cheeks. 'If you could only see your face. I'm sorry. I didn't mean to scare you. Only my own ego's been a bit fragile lately and—well, and I really didn't want to damage anyone else's. But of course I should have known . . . Anyway, I'll be happy to go out with you tomorrow. No strings.'

'No strings,' agreed Henry, looking as if he had escaped a fate much worse than marriage. 'I'll pick you up at seven. Maybe we should take in a movie.'

He was as good as his word. He picked her up at seven and they drove into Vancouver to see a Robin Williams comedy at which they laughed uproariously. By the time Rosemary got home at midnight she was in a more peaceful, relaxed frame of mind than she had been in all week. Maybe she couldn't have Jonathan, but somehow life would go on without him. Because it had to.

And then the telephone rang.

It was Tamsin. At first the high-pitched, childish voice was almost incoherent. When Rosemary was eventually able to distinguish words, she gathered that something had happen to Jonathan.

'Tamsin. Talk slowly. Try to tell me *exactly* what has happened.'

There was a moist, gulping noise on the end of the line, and then a very small voice said quickly, but quite clearly, 'It's Dad. I think he's had an accident.'

Rosemary gripped the edge of the counter as a great wave of nausea swept over her. Then she breathed, and asked as calmly as she could, 'What sort of an accident?'

'I think he fell. He's lying on the kitchen floor, and he's not moving.'

'Is he breathing?'

'Yes. Quite loudly.'

'Hmm,' said Rosemary, as the nausea subsided and the

germ of a supicion began to form in her mind. 'Is anyone with you?'

'No. Debbie was over, but she left fifteen minutes ago and I didn't know what to do. So I called you.'

In the midst of her anxiety, Rosemary, was touched that the girl's first thought had been to get in touch with *her*. But this was no time for sentiment, even though she now had a strong idea that perhaps the situation was not as urgent as she had at first assumed.

'Listen, Tamsin. I'll be right over, but it will take twenty minutes at least. In the meantime, you call Mrs Whitehead. If there's any emergency, she'll be able to help.'

'All right,' agreed Tamsin. 'Thanks, Miss Reid.'

Twenty-two minutes later Rosemary swerved up in front of the Riordan house. She had no difficulty in finding it, because in a moment of curiosity after she had first met Jonathan she had looked up the address in the phone book and driven past.

The kitchen seemed to be full of Whiteheads. One large, balding, black-bearded man, a swarm of burly sons, and Mrs Whitehead, who was small, grey-haired, and seemed to be coping with the crisis in spite of the noise, conflicting instructions and general bumbling about of her menfolk.

The crisis himself was lying on the floor in a slightly rumpled suit, and there was a strong smell of whisky in the room.

As Tamsin led Rosemary into the kitchen, Mrs Whitehead was issuing orders in a surprisingly carrying voice. 'Now, then, you lot. Now, then. Stop all that noise and shoving, and pick him up and get him into bed. There's nothing the matter with him that a good night's sleep won't cure.'

The Whitehead men quietened immediately as two of them took Jonathan by the shoulders and two more seized his legs. A few minutes later his large body was sprawled across the big double bed he must once have shared with Janet.

'Right,' said Mrs Whitehead. 'Now, you lot clear out. You'll only get in the way.'

Jack Whitehead shuffled, and muttered something to the effect that she couldn't undress young Riordan by herself.

'Rubbish. If you think I don't know what a man's body looks like after twenty-five years of you and five sons, you're out of your mind, Jack Whitehead. Miss Reid here and I can manage very well.'

It did not seem to occur to her that young Miss Reid had *not* been putting up with the Whitehead clan for twenty-five years, and might find the thought of undressing her pupil's father embarrassing. In fact, Rosemary found it intimidating all right—but also disturbingly exciting.

Together she and Mrs Whitehead removed Jonathan's jacket and trousers, unbuttoned his shirt to expose the bare, blonde-haired chest below, and finally came to his briefs. When Mrs Whitehead began briskly to remove these as well, Rosemary closed her eyes.

A few minutes later Jonathan was settled in bed, now clad discreetly in dark blue, very unused-looking pyjamas, efficiently unearthed and put on by Mrs Whitehead, while Rosemary, still with her eyes closed, tried to manoevre his big body into suitable positions. By the time they had finished, Rosemary's face was a very bright pink, and she was breathing rather hard.

'There,' said Mrs Whitehead. 'He'll be all right in the morning. Bit of a sore head perhaps, and that's no more than he deserves. What you and I deserve is a nice cup of coffee, my dear. Don't you think so?'

Rosemary agreed, and soon she and Mrs Whitehead were seated at the kitchen table, nursing mugs of coffee and chatting as if they had known each other all their lives. Tamsin came in wearing large leather gloves and clutching something small, sable-coloured and furry. It had a long, dark, bushy tail.

'Meet Dracula,' she said, holding the animal out to Rosemary. Unthinkingly, Rosemary put out her hand to touch it, and was rewarded by a sharp nip on the knuckles.

Mrs Whitehead chuckled. 'Now you're one of the family,' she remarked. 'That little demon has had all of us for a snack at one time or another.'

'I wish you *were* one of the family, Miss Reid,' said Tamsin a little sadly.

Rosemary smiled uncomfortably. 'That's nice of you, Tamsin.' She hesitated and then added, 'I still think you're an unusual young lady, though, to want your teacher for a mother.'

'Yes, but Dad's much nicer when he's happy,' said Tamsin simply, causing Rosemary's heart to turn a somersault. 'Is he going to be OK?'

'Perfectly OK,' Mrs Whitehead assured her.

'He's just drunk, isn't he?' said Tamsin disapprovingly. 'At first I thought he was hurt.'

'I think he stumbled over something—his own feet, probably—and hit his head on the table as he fell,' mused Rosemary. 'There's a bit of a bump on his forehead. But yes, mostly he's just drunk.'

'He's never been drunk before,' objected Tamsin, the disapproval in her voice combing unhappily with anxiety.

Rosemary doubted that. Jonathan was the kind of man

who must have sown plenty of wild oats in his time. But
she did believe he had had the good sense to stay sober in
front of his daughter.

'Did something upset him, then?' she asked cautiously.

'I don't know. He's been grumpy every since Long
Beach. Then tonight he went out with Deloraine again.
She was smarming all over him when they left,' said
Tamsin disgustedly.

'Oh.' Rosemary stared dismally at the table.

'Yes, but he came back early, making an awful noise
and swearing. Then I heard him mutter something about it
being the first time he'd ever turned down an offer from a
doll like Deloraine, and it was all the fault of that damn
little blonde with the freckles and golden-brown eyes.
Then he kicked something—hard—and I heard him fall
over.'

'Oh, dear.' Rosemary lifted her head, met Mrs
Whitehead's gaze fixed on her face with more than an
casual interest, and turned awkwardly away. She found
herself staring into two small smudgy eyes behind a
hopeful pink mouth.

'Dracula looks hungry,' she remarked, changing the
subject quickly.

She's always hungry,' agreed Tamsin. 'I guess I'll feed
her before I go to bed. If you're sure Dad will be OK . . .'

'I'm sure,' said Rosemary grimly. 'But I'll take a look at
him before I go if you like.'

'Good idea,' nodded Mrs Whitehead, standing up. 'I'll
be off, then. It's been a pleasure, Rosemary. At least,
meeting *you* has been a pleasure,' she amended. 'Not
getting that great idiot off the floor. Some men don't
know to hang on to a good thing when they've got one.'

With which cryptic remark she pulled on a faded yellow

cardigan and hurried back to her noisy crew next door.

Rosemary made her way upstairs.

Jonathan was lying on his back, breathing quite evenly now. The blue-patterned bedspread which he had obviously not bothered to change since Janet's day was pushed down to his waist and shimmered faintly in the light from the window. Rosemary stared at the wide, masculine chest and the powerful arms flung carelessy across the sheets. One hand was curled around a corner of the bedspread, creasing it into a ball.

Very carefully, Rosemary moved towards him. He was all right now. There was no need to disturb him. But when she reached the side of the bed she could not resist putting out her hand to remove the crumpled fabric from his fingers.

She was so intent on her task, and on not waking him up, that it was complete shock when his other hand closed suddenly around her wrist, and she found herself gazing into smoke-grey eyes not three inches from her own.

# CHAPTER TEN

'WELL, well, well,' murmured Jonathan. 'So the night is mine, after all.'

'Like hell it is,' hissed Rosemary, trying to extricate her wrist, and failing. 'Last time we met you accused me of teaching a course in Group Groping—so you can just forget about groping me, Jonathan Riordan.'

'Can I? Then what are you doing in my bed?'

'I'm not in it, I'm beside it.'

'Well, we can soon remedy that, can't we?'

One powerful arm shot out and locked around her waist. The ugly bedside lamp with its shade of frills and bows teetered precariously on its perch, and Rosemary, for one ridiculous second distracted from more immediate concerns, wondered why Jonathan had not long ago removed these relics of Janet's florid taste. Then she stopped caring as she found that she was lying on top of him with the tips of her shoes suspended just above the floor.

He released her arm to place his big hand at the back of her head. Their faces were almost touching, and the smell of whisky was very faint now, and rather pleasant. Rosemary held her breath, transfixed and unable to move. Then, as a realisation of what was happening to her crept into her paralysed brain, she stirred and tried to pull away.

Jonathan's hand slid down from her waist to move

slowly, sensuously over the blue silk trousers covering her
bottom.

'Don't fight me,' he murmured, pressing her close. 'I
didn't mean to accuse you of anything, you know. I was
just being the heavy father that time on the beach. Forgive
me?'

He pulled her head down on his shoulder, and she
found she had no will to move it. 'Of course I forgive
you.'

He blew softly behind her ear, and in a moment she felt
his lips against her neck. And his fingers were trailing
deliriously up her sides.

'No!' cried Rosemary, making a desperate effort to free
herself, and struggling to sit up. 'No, Jonathan.'

He let her go and she perched nervously on the edge of
the bed, a bird poised for flight, and with her eyes fixed
warily on Jonathan's hands.

'Why not?' The smile he gave her set every pulse in her
body pounding, and she drew herself even closer to the
edge.

'Because—we can't—Tamsin . . .'

'Tamsin's asleep. Listen.'

Rosemary listened, and faintly through the walls she
heard the sound of gentle snoring.

'And you're drunk,' she continued desperately.

'I'm not in the least bit drunk.' He reached suddenly
towards he and caught her hand in his.

'But you have been drinking,' she argued, pulling
quickly away. 'And you fell. You hit your head.' As
though she couldn't stop herself, she leaned over to touch
the purple shading on his forehead. 'It's all mauve and
mottled.'

'I must be a charming sight.' The firm mouth so close to

hers broke into a grin. 'But don't worry about it. Mauve's in this year.' He lunged at her again and caught her around the waist. 'Sure I've been drinking. You drove me to it. And now you're going to pay.' Laughing triumphantly, his mouth closed over hers and he pulled her down beside him on the bed.

For a moment Rosemary struggled, and then, as his tongue forced itself between her lips and she felt the strength of his body through the thin blue silk of her blouse, she knew she didn't want to fight him any more. She returned his kiss with all the love that was in her heart, and she tasted a warmth and sweetness she had never known before.

And she was willing to pay his price.

Then she felt his fingers tug at the buttons of her blouse. At the same time the wind rose suddenly and whipped a branch against the window—and reality came crushing about her ears. From the corner of her eyes she caught a glimpse of the frilly lampshade. She drew in her breath—and smelled again the tantalising maleness of his body. For one timeless moment she hesitated, Then with a low, unconscious murmur, she wrenched herself away and stumbled to her feet.

'No!' she cried. 'No, please, Jonathan . . .'

His grey eyes were very steady, regarding her with a look that held more than frustrated passion. There was an emotion reflected in those slate-grey depths that she could not begin to understand. And in the end she couldn't bear to look and she turned her head away.

'What is it, Rosemary?' he asked quietly. She looked up and saw a sudden flicker of surprised speculation cross his face and he asked disbelievingly, 'You're not . . .?'

'No,' said Rosemary honestly. 'I'm not. But it's been a

long time . . .'

'Then why . . .?'

Now that he was not quite so disturbingly close, Rosemary found common sense returning. 'Because,' she replied tartly, 'I expected to marry Ronald. And as you made arrogantly clear that last day over at Long Beach, I needn't waste any of my time expecting to marry you.'

He stared at her, and in his eyes there were something shuttered and still. 'Was I arrogant?'

'Incredibly.'

'Mm.' He was still lying flat on the bed, but now he pushed himself up to rest with his back against the headboard. 'I suppose I was,' he admitted finally. 'And you were a scratchy little vixen. Just like the first time I met you.' He smiled at her, but it was a strained, weary sort of smile, and Rosemary felt something cold and hard tighten unhappily around her chest.

'If I was scratchy, it was only because you hurt me,' she told him tiredly.

'Did I? Sometimes the truth does hurt, Rosemary. And it is the truth that I can never love again.' His voice was deep, and very bitter. 'For that small mercy I think you may one day be grateful. My love would only bring you grief.'

'Perhaps I should be the judge of that.' Rosemary's voice too was edged with bitterness as she stared down at this half-naked man who but a moment before had been urging her to share his bed, and had now become a cool, reserved stranger.

'Yes. Perhaps you should. In fact, I thought you had.'

'Had what?'

'Judged me and found me lacking. What was it you said? That I had nothing to give you that you wanted?'

Absently Rosemary tucked her blouse into her waistband and ran a hand through her hair. 'Did you believe me?'

'No.'

'Then why didn't you get in touch with me? Is there some reason we can't be—friends?'

He wasn't looking at her now, and abruptly he swung his long legs out of the bed and stood up. 'There's every reason in the world,' he said walking over to the window and flinging it open to the night. 'I want you, Rosemary. I think you want me too. And anything less would be—more than either of us could endure.'

'Oh, would it?' said Rosemary, her confusion and unhappiness rapidly becoming submerged by indignation. 'You have a remarkable opinion of yourself, Jonathan Riordan, if you think I can't come near you without wanting to make passionate love to your admittedly quite impressive body.'

He turned to face her and a small, twisted smile flicked the corner of his lips.

'*Touché,*' he murmured quietly.

Something in his calm, withdrawn acceptance of her rebuke quite suddenly touched Rosemary's heart, and she took a quick step towards him before bringing herself up short.

'Jonathan,' she implored him, 'Don't torment me any more. You're right. The truth can hurt and I do want you. More than I've ever wanted anyone or anything in my life. But why must you be so—so warm and wonderful one minute—and like a—a predatory panther the next? First you told me it wasn't fair to use me when you had nothing to give in return. Then tonight you tried to do just that . . .'

'You weren't almost in my bed that other time.' His back was to her again and he was leaning on the windowsill, his shoulders somehow broader and more massive against the moonlight. 'Have you any idea what it did to me, waking up from a pleasantly alcoholic dream to find you bending over me—in pale, slinky silk with your beautiful hair in my face? In the moonlight. It was like every man's fantasy come true, Rosemary. And I am very much every man.'

No, you're not, thought Rosemary in silent anguish. You're *not* every man. You're an impossible, fascinating, very special man. The only man I want. She dug her nails hard into her palms. And you're also the one you tell me I can never, ever have.

But she didn't say it. Instead she gazed at his back and at the sinuous forearms pressed against the sill, and wondered if this was the end.

After a long time he turned around, and the light gleamed golden on his burnished hair. 'I'm sorry,' he said, in a voice that had gone flat and toneless. He took a quick step forward and then gestured dismissively at the door. 'I don't know what you're doing here. And as I have no wish to torment you, perhaps you had better go.'

Just like that. Grief and fury rose like twin demons in Rosemary's throat, and through a blaze of pain she heard herself shouting at him, 'You bastard! You think I'm just one of your gold-diggers, don't you? Good for a bit of fun, a quick roll in the sheets, but nothing permanent. Oh, no! Not for Jonathan Riordan who can have any woman he wants and love 'em and leave 'em at will.' She threw her head back scornfully. 'And because you can't have me on those terms, you pretend to an undying devotion to your Janet—with her frills and fringes and flowery furniture.' She waved a hand around the fussily furnished room. 'All these years, and the bedroom's still hers, isn't it? Why,

Jonathan? To ward off the evil spirit of commitment—and love?' Her voice, which had risen **to** wake the dead—or at least poor Tamsin, she thought with sudden guilt—faded in a dying fall as she came to the word 'love', and she turned blindly towards the door.

But, as she reached out for the handle, she felt Jonathan's hand grip her upper arm as she was spun around to face him. And his eyes in the moonlight were hypnotic and dark and frightening. She tried to back away, but his grip only tightened.

'All right, Rosemary,' he bit out, through lips which were so hard that she could not believe they had ever been soft and gentle against her own. 'All right. You believe that if you want to. But don't you ever, and I mean ever, speak about my wife like that again. Her taste may not be your taste. But she made a home for me. And I loved her—once . . .' His voice was the edge of a knife, cutting and bladed like steel. But she was the one who had drawn blood.

Rosemary heard the pain, and saw the anger in his eyes, and suddenly she could bear it no longer. Oh, God, what had she done to him? What, in her own despair, had she said to this man she loved?'

With a small, wounded cry she groped for the handle of the door, opened it and stumbled unseeingly down the darkened stairs.

'Wait!' She heard Jonathan's voice crack sharply behind her as she ran.

But Rosemary didn't wait. She pushed open the door, ran into the street where the night air pulled the breath from her lungs, and leaped desperately into her car.

Luckily there were few other cars on the road as she drove like a fiend to Richmond, and it was not until she had slumped down at her kitchen table to bury her face in her hands that the full knowledge of what she had lost came over her again, and she knew a black despair that hit her like a blast of freezing wind. Because she understood that as an antidote to her own pain she had said terrible things to Jonathan. Perhaps they were partly true. She honestly didn't know. But to use his dead wife as a weapon with which to wound him—that had been unforgivable.

Hours later she lifted her head from the table, her body stiff and chilled through, and saw that it was morning.

The next few weeks passed by in a strangely blank blur. Rosemary went to school, cleaned out cages of gerbils, rats and iguanas with almost ferocious thoroughness, attended a concert with Henry, a party with John from the lab and, in the extended spring evenings, often took Murphy and Muffin for long, frenetic walks along the dyke. In a moment of abstraction—she was always abstracted these days—she even went out and bought the sexy red track-suit Jonathan had expected her to own. But when she put it on she decided it wasn't sexy at all, and only made her look like a lumpy, pyjama-clad pillar-box. She didn't want to jog, in any case. There were other, less frantic ways of keeping busy and healthy. Ways which might have the added advantage of leaving her no time to think.

Easter came and went, and Rosemary spent the holidays with her parents in Kelowna. She saw Ronald again and was not at all surprised to discover that his proximity had no effect on her at all. But if he wanted to be friendly that was quite all right with her. And if it happened that she never saw him again—well, that was all right too.

But behind all Rosemary's activity and determined occupation there was a small, cold, heavy lump in her chest, a leaden cloud which hung over her spirits and refused to let her be—because, although she didn't know why Jonathan was so adamantly convinced that he could never love again, she did know that after the things she had said to him at their last meeting, if he ever gave his heart again, it would surely not be to her.

Shortly after Easter, Tamsin caught up with her in the hall as she was heading to the staffroom for lunch.

'Miss Reid,' the girl gasped breathlessly, 'Miss Reid, can I talk to you for a minute?'

Rosemary paused. 'Sure. I can eat my lunch in the biology office as well as anywhere else.' She turned back the way she had come. 'What about your lunch, Tamsin?'

Tamsin shook her head. 'I tried to eat it, but it just wouldn't go down.'

'Oh.' Rosemary glanced at the pale face beside her worriedly. It was drawn and strained, as it had been for the last few weeks.

'What's the trouble, Tamsin?' she asked, as they sat down on two folding chairs besides Rosemary's cluttered desk.

'It's Dad,' explained Tamsin. 'He's been stamping about the house like the Ghost of Christmas Yet to Come lately—you know, with an awful empty face, and you can almost see that long, black, gloomy cloak around him. I don't know what do about it.'

'Oh, dear,' said Rosemary. 'What's the matter, do you think?'

'I don't know,' replied Tamsin sadly. 'I thought it might be you.' She twisted a strand of hair through her fingers. 'He's taken up sky-diving again, too.'

'Sky-diving!' Rosemary almost yelped.

'Mm. He did that for a while after mother died as well.

Until Uncle Derek told him it wasn't fair to me because he was all I had left.'

'Then you'd better get Uncle Derek to talk to him again.'

'He has. But Dad says I'm almost seventeen now, and off to university next year. Besides, he doesn't really believe it's dangerous.'

'No,' agreed Rosemary crossly. 'I suppose your father thinks he's immortal.'

'He does, I expect. But the way he's acting now, I'm not sure he wants to be.'

Rosemary eyed her meditatively. 'I suppose you couldn't persuade him to take up golf instead?'

Tamsin sighed. 'No. And besides, the way he's been lately, he'd probably step in front of the first bad shot he saw coming and get himself hit on the head.'

'Might do him some good,' muttered Rosemary under her breath.

But Tamsin heard her, and for the first time that day she smiled. 'Yes, it might,' she agreed. 'Miss Reid . . .?'

'Yes?'

'*Is* my Dad in this brooding bad temper over you?'

Rosemary shook her head. 'I doubt it, she said quietly. 'And it doesn't sound to me as if he's brooding much at all. Sky-diving isn't brooding.'

'No, I suppose not. Only—I didn't hear what you actually said, but I couldn't help hearing you and Dad shouting at each other that night. So I just wondered . . .'

'Oh, dear, did you?' Thank God the girl *hadn't* heard what was said. Rosemary found herself shuddering at the thought.

'Yes, I did,' Tamsin assured her. 'But come to think of it, I guess it must be something else that's making Dad so grumpy. Because he could see you again if he wanted to, couldn't he, Miss Reid?'

'Oh, yes,' said Rosemary up and walking over to the sink. 'He could see me again if he wanted to.' She turned the tap on a specimen jar and splashed water all over the floor.

It was only after Tamsin had left and they had agreed that Jonathan would have to battle his demons in his own way that Rosemary heard the bell ring for class and realised she had forgotten to eat her lunch.

That night she ran one hand over Muffin's silky fur, and after a long time reached the other one slowly towards the phone. Then she drew back. She couldn't call him. It wasn't only pride, or the fear of rejection. It was just that she knew if by some stroke of magic Jonathan did not hang up on her, eventually it would all work out the same.

He had said he could never love again. That meant that sooner or later he would turn away from her once more—and she would have to cope with a loss which would be that much harder to bear. And she couldn't face that. Not for a few brief moments of joy which she knew would be snatched away to torture her with all that she had missed.

So Rosemary didn't call, and the plum trees changed from pink to leafy green, and Murphy and Muffin chased ducks beside the Fraser as the days grew longer and warmer and the sun rose high in the sky.

It was the beginning of June before she emerged from the mists of her own misery to notice that Tamsin was even more wan and pale than usual, and that she had developed a slight twitch in one eye.

'Aren't you well, Tamsin?' she asked worriedly, annoyed with herself for being so absorbed in her own problems that she had failed to see what might be an even bigger problem beneath her nose.

'I'm all right,' murmured Tamsin. 'I've got a bit of a headache, that's all.'

But the following day Tamsin didn't turn up for biology, and when Rosemary enquired, she was informed that the girl had almost passed out in Mr Parkinson's mathematics class, and had been sent home for the day.

Tamsin was away for the rest of the week. When she was still absent the following Monday, Rosemary became alarmed. Suddenly her own unhappiness was not important any more. But when she asked the office when Tamsin would be back, they said they didn't know. Apparently her father had phoned to tell them she had 'flu, but that was all they had heard.

As soon as she got home that night, Rosemary hurried over to see Alice.

'Has Derek told you anything about Tamsin?' she asked tht old lady anxiously.

But Alice shook her head. 'No,' she said, in a voice of deepest disgust. 'All Derek can talk about is Bozo. She's back from Zimbabwe, off to Bangladesh next week, and in between she's getting married.'

Rosemary blinked. 'To Derek?' she asked, momentarily distracted from her worry about Tamsin.

'To Derek.' Alice's normally cheerful old face screwed up until it resembled a disapproving prune. 'The wedding is on Saturday.'

'Oh.' Rosemary didn't know what to say. 'Are you going to it?'

'To the wedding? Suppose so. He is my only nephew— even if he has less sense than all of my tollers put together. At least they don't mate for life—to people with names like Bozo.'

Rosemary's lips twitched. 'Perhaps they would if you gave them a chance,' she suggested. 'Besides—well, would you marry a man called Muffin?'

Alice let out a crack of laughter. 'Wouldn't marry any man, my dear.' She shot Rosemary a sharp look. 'But you should. Wish it had been Derek, but . . .' She shrugged. 'Well, that's not to be, is it? Young fool missed the chance of a lifetime when he let that conniving boyfriend of yours talk him into indigestion.'

'Jonathan's not my boyfriend, Alice.'

'Hm.' Alice eyed her shrewdly. 'Ought to be, then. He's a fool if he doesn't know it. Bad as my nephew. Don't hold out much hope for that company of theirs—run by a couple of idiots.' She sighed, and added glumly, 'I've got shares in it, too.'

Rosemary laughed. Alice could always lighten her mood. 'I suppose you'll be seeing—Jonathan—at the wedding?' she asked carefully.

'Don't know. Suppose so. Not if his daughter's ill, though. Why don't you phone him?'

Yes, thought Rosemary when she got home. Why don't I? It wasn't a matter of getting in touch with Jonathan for herself. It was just that she wanted—needed—to know about Tamsin.

She stared at the black phone crouched on the edge of the counter. It seemed to be daring her to touch it. She went on staring for a long time, and then she picked it up.

'Yes?' Jonathan's tone was abrupt, but it sent a jolt of tingling warmth down Rosemary's spine as she pictured his tall body lounging against the counter in his kitchen —or lying back in bed with those hands which had once curled around her body now curled about the receiver.

She swallowed, and then announced briskly, in her best

'Miss Reid' voice, 'It's Rosemary. I was just wondering how Tamsin was.'

There was a long silence. Just when she had decided he must have hung up, his answer cracked back long the wire.

'Tamsin's all right. Is that all you wanted?'

As so often happened when she talked to Jonathan, Rosemary felt her hackles rising. 'No, it is *not* all I want. Your daughter had been away for over a week, she's missed a lot of work, and I'm concerned about her. Is she really sick? And when will she be back?'

'The answer to both your questions is "I don't know". The twitch in her eye has gone, but she still has headaches, mild stomach cramps and no energy whatever.'

'But it's not appendicitis?'

'Why should it be?' Behind the natural anxiety of a father for his ailing child, his irritation was palpable.

Rosemary sighed. 'I don't know. You mentioned stomach cramps, and my life seems to have been haunted by appendicitis lately.'

When he answered, Rosemary detected a faint lightening in his tone, almost as though he were tempted to laugh, but was damned if he was going to.

'No, it's not her appendix, ghostly or otherwise. The doctor doesn't seem to know what it is. But she's seeing a specialist next week, if she hasn't improved by then.'

'I see. Is there someone with her while you're at work, then?'

'Of course.' The impatience was back. 'Contrary to your unflattering opinion of me, I'm not a complete fool, Rosemary. Either Mrs Peacock or Mrs Whitehead is with her all the time.'

'That's good. And I know you're not a fool.' Rosemary hesitated, played with the telephone cord, and finally said all in a rush, 'Do you think I could come and see her?'

This time the silence seemed never-ending. When at last he broke it, it was to say harshly, almost angrily, 'I don't think that will be necessary.'

'No, but . . .'

'And I don't think it's a good idea.'

Rosemary gazed blankly at the bright curtains blowing in the breeze from the window, and found that she couldn't see them properly because a mist had formed over her eyes.

'All right,' she whispered into the receiver. 'Give Tamsin my love. Goodbye, Jonathan.'

Blindly she hung up the phone and stumbled over to the table. This was really the end, then. She would never see Jonathan again. Tamsin would probably get well in no time. Teenagers were resilient. But she, Rosemary, would spend the rest of her life alone.

When Murphy scratched at the door half a hour later, several minutes passed by before she even heard him.

# CHAPTER ELEVEN

THE next day Rosemary was late getting home from school. She had lingered behind on purpose, partly to clear up some end-of-term marking, but mainly because she couldn't face the prospect of spending the evening at home in her quiet house with nothing to do but think.

Now, as she pulled into her driveway, she wished she had been less hasty in declining John's invitation to join him and a group of friends at one of the local night-clubs. When he had asked her, she had been feeling so despondent that she had been sure she would cast a pall of gloom over the entire party. But the alternative was sitting at home alone . . .

She brushed a hand quickly across her eyes, sighed, and climbed out of the Toyota.

A yellow sports car which she vaguely recognised was parked in front of the house next door, and as she reached for an armful of books on the seat two figures emerged from Alice's front door and started to walk towards it.

'Rosemary!' Alice caught sight of her young neighbour and waved. 'Come over here a minute. I want you to meet my nephew.'

Slowly Rosemary crossed the intervening grass. A tall, dark man in his mid-thirties was smiling down at her. He had a cheerful, friendly face and his bright eyes surveyed her with unconcealed interest.

'So you're the one who's been getting me into so much

glue lately,' he grinned. 'Well, now that I see what all the fuss is about, I guess I'm not surprised.'

Rosemary smiled back uncertainly. 'Glue?' she enquired.

'Mm. The sticky stuff comes from my Aunt Alice here, who thinks Bozo is an unsuitable name for a wife, and from my bull-headed partner who's been impossible to work with since he did me out of my introduction to you in the first place.'

'You did that to yourself, my lad,' snapped Alice. 'You had no reason whatever to let him have his way.'

'Yes, I had. Her name's Bozo.' Derek's eyes twinkled teasingly at his aunt, and she clicked her tongue impatiently.

Rosemary looked doubtfully from one to the other. 'I understand congratulations are in order,' she said formally to Derek.

'Indeed they are. Now if we could just do the same for my partner, it might become possible to work with him again without getting one's head bitten off for breathing. And Tamsin might get better.'

'What?' Rosemary stared at him. 'What do you mean, Tamsin might get better?'

'Just what I say. If you ask me, which of course nobody has, that young lady's problems are emotional.'

'But—she did have 'flu . . .'

'Sure she did. But she should have recovered weeks ago. I'm just not sure she wants to.'

'Yes, but . . .' Rosemary studied his face intently and saw only sincerity on the wide blue eyes. 'I suppose you could be right. Only—what do you think is upsetting her? Is it . . .?' She couldn't bring herself to say his name.

'Yes, it's Jonathan,' Derek finished for her. 'Also, I

think she wants to see you.'

'Me? But Jonathan doesn't want . . .'

'Jonathan doesn't know what he wants. No. That's not true. He knows all right, but he's too damned obstinate to admit it.'

'Hm. Sounds like someone else I know,' interrupted Alice.

Derek wagged his finger at her. 'I know exactly what I want, Aunt Alice. and I'm afraid her name's still Bozo.'

Rosemary saw the ghost of a smile flit across Alice's wrinkled features. 'You always were as stubborn as a ostrich,' muttered the old lady.

'An ostrich?' Derek passed a hand across his mouth. 'Well, if you say so. But old Johnno's as stubborn and thick as rhinoceros hide.'

'Why do you say that?' asked Rosemary carefully, running her hand over the smoothness of Derek's shining yellow car-top, and hoping he couldn't read her eyes.

'Because, Miss Rosemary Reid, my old friend Johnno's so busy shielding himself from commitment behind a wall of his own past sins, that he's decided to cut off his nose to spite his face. Oh, he'll enjoy the odd casual fling with some ghastly female with long legs, curves and a sexy . . .'

'Derek!' Alice's sharp voice snapped through the evening air.

Derek grinned and finished quickly, 'But he refuses to have anything to do with women who might want him for himself, instead of for what he can give them.'

Well, he had plenty to do with me, thought Rosemary involuntarily. But aloud she only said, 'Why?' in a very low voice which broke suddenly into a croak.

'Because of Janet,' replied Derek. 'She used to go on at him about leaving her alone so much, though he really couldn't help it. We were just starting up the business. All the same, he wanted to make her happy. Then she died.'

'What happened to her, Derek?' Rosemary was almost afraid to ask.

'She had a heart attack. Some congenital weakness that had never been detected. But unfortunately it happened when Jonathan was out meeting a client. It was quite late in the evening, and apparently he had promised to take Janet for a special birthday dinner. When the client called, he broke the date. Janet was furious and told him not to go. But that was a mistake, because nobody tells old Johnno what to do. So he went. When he came home, she was lying on the bedroom floor. She'd been dead for several hours.'

'Oh, poor Jonathan,' whispered Rosemary, covering her face with her hands. 'And of course he blamed himself.'

'Of course. He felt responsible, because her last hours weren't happy ones—and because she died. Although in this case, I doubt if there was anything he could have done. The autopsy concluded it was very sudden. In fact, Tamsin slept right through it. Didn't even hear her mother fall.'

'Thank God.'

'Yes. But I'm afraid it's left my impossible partner with a firm conviction that he's not good marriage material. He couldn't save Janet because he wasn't there, so he insists that any woman who is misguided enough to love him is bound to be the loser. Perhaps that's just his way of avoiding any involvements, but—I don't know. It's true he was quite protective about Janet at one time—and in the end he couldn't protect her at all.' Derek pushed his hair back off his forehead and then, surprisingly, grinned as he added, 'I've told him he should settle for somebody like Bozo. Nobody in their right mind could possibly think she's in need of protection.'

'Huh. Because she's never there to be protected,' snorted Alice.

'Now, now, Aunt Alice,' admonished Derek. 'Don't be disagreeable. Bozo's a very fine woman.' He turned back to Rosemary. 'Anyway, that's the sad story of my partner Johnno. But it's too bad for little Tamsin. I think she had real hopes that her father had found someone permanent at last. Someone they could both love. She wants to see him happy more than anything else. And in spite of what he says, I don't believe he is. But Tamsin also needs a mother—who can sometimes be a friend. Now I think she's just suffering from depression. In fact, their household at the moment is about as cheerful as a plague-pit.' His eyes searched Rosemary's face. 'And I suppose you're the fatal female behind all this gloom and doom— although neither of them has said so.'

Rosemary shook her head. 'No. Oh, no. I couldn't be.' She brushed a non-existent hair away from her eyes. 'It's been nice talking to you, Mr—Derek. Give my love to Tamsin, and—and to . . . Yes. Well, I'll be seeing you, Alice. Thanks for . . . Goodnight.'

Without really knowing where she was going, Rosemary turned around and ran back across the grass. But when she found herself outside her own front door, she knew she couldn't bear to go inside just yet.

The door of the Toyota still hung open. She slammed it shut, ran across the little bridge in front of her house, along the curving, bumpy road, past houses, farms and fields until, hours later, and without quite knowing how she got there, she fetched up alone and exhausted on the southern dyke.

She was miles from home, with the evening drawing in and a summer breeze rippling the grey waters of the Fraser. There was nobody about, not even a dedicated jogger or dog-walker, and Rosemary sat down with her back against a small tree, her bottom in a patch of mud, and stared unseeingly at the flat, wood-strewn strip of stony foreshore below.

So now she knew why Jonathan had told her he wouldn't make the mistake of marrying again. Perhaps, as Derek had suggested, it was just an excuse for remaining single. But, knowing him as she did, she didn't really believe he had ever needed an excuse for doing as he pleased. No, it was probably true that the manner of Janet's death had shaken him to the core. And he had been a younger man then, possibly without the maturity or self-knowledge to cope with the idea that if he had been less absorbed in his own needs Janet might—just might—still be alive. Rosemary had a feeling that Jonathan had always had a streak of arrogance—that it must have been shattering to his perception of himself to find that his decisions where not infallibly right, that in fact this one decision had perhaps been fatal.

She pulled at a blade of grass. It snapped, and thoughtfully she placed it in her mouth and ran it between her teeth. The more she thought about it, though, the more she realised that Jonathan was now a strong, secure and exceedingly confident man. His reluctance to love again might stem in part from the tragedy of his marriage. But it was also entirely possible that he was comfortable as he was, and unwilling to change his free and easy existence for the ups and downs of marriage—which experience had taught him was by no means all roses and moonlight, bed, and someone to cook his breakfast.

Gradually, as she sat there, and the sun sank lower in the sky, Rosemary began to feel the stirrings of a familiar indignation. It was true she had said awful things to him about his feelings for his wife. But Jonathan had no right to stop her seeing Tamsin—just because *he* didn't want to see the woman he had tried to seduce on the night he went out with Deloraine and ended up flaked out on the kitchen floor.

Abruptly Rosemary jumped to her feet. To hell with Jonathan Riordan and his self-protective wall! Tomorrow she would drive to Point Gray immediately after school. And she would visit Tamsin whether he said she could or not.

When she approached the road, Rosemary looked for her car, and remembered that she had left it in her driveway. She glanced at the sky. It would be dark soon, and she was alone on the deserted dyke. Damn! What a fool she had been. And all because of Jonathan Riordan—who didn't want to see her again.

Angry now, with herself as well as him, she tramped down the darkened roadway.

She had only been walking for a few minutes when a car pulled up beside her. She jumped and looked around her for a weapon, then saw the car was a police cruiser.

'You in any trouble, Miss?' asked the young Mountie behind the wheel.

'No, no, really, I . . .' Rosemary glanced down at her white, mud-spattered slacks, put a hand to her untidily blowing hair and gave an embarrassed laugh. No wonder he thought she was in trouble.

'No,' she said more firmly. 'I'm afraid I just forgot the time.'

The young policeman glanced pointedly at her watch and raised his eyebrows. But when she told him where she was heading, he said he was going that way himself and in the end she arrived home in a police car—much to the astonishment of Alice, who was outside calling Muffin.

By the time she got to bed that night, Rosemary was feeling more determined than unhappy—and much more definitely alive than she had been since the last time she had seen Jonathan. Just because of him she had been brought home in a police car. And if he thought for one moment he could stop her seeing Tamsin, he had never been more mistaken in his life.

Rosemary stood with her fingers on the doorbell. She had been waiting on the steps of the house in Point Gray for at least three minutes now, and no one had come to answer her short, discreet rings, although she could have sworn she heard movements inside and the sound of someone coughing.

At last, when she had all but given up, the door flew open and Mrs Whitehead stood there, her grey hair slightly awry, and wearing a pair of gloves.

'Rosemary!' she exclaimed breathlessly. 'Oh, I heard you ring, but that little monster had just escaped again and got into Tamsin's cupboard.' She waved a hand at a small, sable-coloured streak who was darting towards the open door. 'Dracula has already eaten holes in all the bed-spreads, and she's crazy about leather, so I had to get her out. Come on in.'

Closing the door hastily behind her, Rosemary stepped inside. The ferret, thwarted, made a bee-line for the stairs. With a sound like a Highland war-cry, Mrs Whitehead plunged after her, grabbed, and missed and tripped on the bottom step.

Rosemary helped her up and led her into the kitchen. 'Here, sit down,' she urged. 'I'll make you a cup of tea.'

'Oh, thank you. I could use one. But we'd better catch up with the vampire first. Tamsin's asleep, and I don't want her woken up.'

'I'll get her,' said Rosemary firmly, removing the gloves from Mrs Whitehead's hand and mentally damning Jonathan for buying Dracula instead of a nice, unobtrusive Dobermann—or a Great Dane. 'You just sit tight. I'll be back in a minute.'

It was more than a minute by the time she had successfully cornered Dracula in Tamsin's wastepaper basket, and of course by then Tamsin was wide awake—and grinning in delighted disbelief at the sight of Rosemary with tooth marks on her nose, depositing a wriggling Dracula forcibly in her cage and slamming down the lid.

'How did she get out?' were the girl's first puzzled words to Rosemary.

'I don't know. I expect Mrs Whitehead tried to clean the cage. It needs it.'

'I know. I haven't felt like doing it.' Tamsin's big eyes gazed at Rosemary with a look of frustration. Along with something else that looked remarkably like hope.

'Are you and Dad friends again?' she asked.

'I think we've always been friends—sort of. But if you mean more than that—no, I'm afraid nothing has changed. But Tamsin, you and I are still friends. Can you tell me what's been the matter?'

'I don't know . . . I had 'flu, but that's over now. I think I want to get up, but when I try my head starts to hurt . . .'

'Maybe you don't really want to get better?'

'Mm.' Tamsin gave her a small, secretive smile. 'I did think that if I was ill for long enough, Dad might let you come over. I told him I wanted to see you.'

'I'm glad. But—why me, Tamsin?'

Tamsin grinned, her big eyes suddenly alive and mischievous. 'Because Dad wants to see you again, too—whether he knows it or not.'

'Oh.' Rosemary was nonplussed and, seeing her teacher's distressed, unhappy face, Tamsin's eyes, which a moment ago had brimmed with laughter, filled surprisingly with tears.

Dropping quickly to the side of the pink and white bed, Rosemary cradled the girl's head against her breast.

Some time later, when the clanking of cups told Rosemary that Mrs Whitehead had been obliged to make her own tea, Tamsin lifted her head, sniffed, and said she felt much better.

'I'm sure I can get up now,' she said confidently. 'Will you come and see me again, Miss Reid?'

'Yes, of course I will.' Rosemary smiled fondly at the girl and stroked her long brown hair. 'Come on, then. Up you get.'

After her long sojourn in bed, Tamsin was very unsteady on her way down to the kitchen. But she made it in the end, slowly and triumphantly, and Mrs Whitehead, beaming with delight at her young neighbour's probable recovery, handed them both cups of tea. Then the three of them sat down comfortably to talk.

By the time she had consumed three cups of tea and a piece of Mrs Whitehead's excellent lemon cake, Rosemary was feeling relaxed, and very glad she had made the effort to come—in spite of Jonathan's objections. Tamsin's pale face was flushed, but she looked all the better for her trip downstairs.

'I think,' said Rosemary without much enthusiasm, 'that perhaps I should have a go at cleaning Dracula's cage now. Your bedroom will smell much nicer without that charming aroma of musk and dying skunk.'

'Oh, I'll do it,' began Tamsin.

'No need. You don't want to overtire yourself, and I've had a lot of experience cleaning cages. Where do you keep your litter, Tamsin?'

'In the basement.'

'OK.' Leaving the other two at the table, Rosemary went upstairs and, praying fervently that Dracula would keep her vampire activities to a minimum, removed her from the cage and placed her on the floor. Then she made a mad dash through the door with the cage precariously balanced on one arm, and just succeeded in preventing another jail-break as Dracula, making a soft nattering noise, feinted sideways at the opening.

Ten minutes later, with the plastic cage cleaned and sweet-smelling, Rosemary returned it to Tamsin's room. Then she looked around hopefully for its intended occupant who, of course, was nowhere to be seen.

'Come on, Dracula,' she crooned. 'Nice girl. There's a good ferret. Come to Mama, there's a girl.' When these blandishments brought no response, she continued crossly, 'Dracula, you hairy horror, come on out. No, sorry. I didn't mean that. Nice horr . . . I mean, nice ferret. Come on, girl. Dracula . . .?'

There was still no response, so she got down on all fours and peered underneath the bed. All she could see was a moth-eaten collection of slippers that looked as though they should have been decently interred years ago, and three grubby plates. There was something congealed, and quite possibly alive, stuck unpleasantly to their rims.

'Yuck,' said Rosemary, dropping the bedspread quickly—and then, as something furry and flying landed on her upturned bottom, ran up her back and nipped her neatly on the neck, *'Ouch!'*

Behind her she heard a faint sound and, as she started to turn around, a well-known voice that had not lost its power to curl her toes and turn her knees to mush, said clearly and very deliberately, 'What the *hell* do you think you're doing in my daughter's bedroom, cooing sweet inanities at an empty room—and presenting that most delectable backside to the world?'

# CHAPTER TWELVE

ROSEMARY stopped turning and stayed exactly where she was, with both hands on the floor and the neat gold gaberdine bottom in question pointed awkwardly in the air.

'Very tempting,' the voice behind her murmured drily.

Rosemary scrambled hastily to her feet, her hands, knees and hair all covered in dust, and stared defiantly at Jonathan.

'I'm visiting your daughter,' she informed him.

'Under the bed?' The steady grey eyes fixed impersonally on hers held no hint of amusement, yet something quivered in his voice, and Rosemary studied his face intently for some sign that he was not as displeased to see her as he looked. But she couldn't find it.

'No, not under the bed,' she snapped. 'Tamsin's in the kitchen with Mrs Whitehead, as I've no doubt you're perfectly well aware. I was looking for Dracula, if you must know.'

'I'd say you've found her,' he remarked, gesturing at Rosemary's neck.

She gave an exasperated sigh. 'I know, but she's gone again.'

'No, she hasn't, she's eating my shoe.' Jonathan bent down and picked up the slippery little animal, and with one swift movement dumped her firmly in the newly cleaned cage and closed the lid.

'There. Now, can we please get down to business?'

'Business?'

Jonathan's strong jaw hardened and he took a step towards her so that his tall figure seemed to tower over hers. Rosemary looked up at him and caught her breath, fighting an unthinkable urge to put her hands in his hair and pull his large head down to hers. But he was speaking in a low, controlled voice, and his tone did not encourage intimacy.

'Yes, business,' he repeated. 'Why are you here, Rosemary? I told you not to come.'

She lifted her chin scornfully. 'I know you did—and all you were thinking about was yourself—as usual. If you'd given a damn about Tamsin's feelings, you would have known she wanted to see me.' Then she added in a quieter voice, 'But to tell the truth, I didn't think you would be here.'

'Didn't you now? I happen to live here, you know.'

His voice was without warmth, and Rosemary replied equally coolly. 'Yes, I do know. But I thought you'd still be at work.'

'I see. Well, I came home early. And I'd very much like to know what you're doing—sneaking around my house like a thief in the middle of the night.'

'Oh, don't be ridiculous!' replied Rosemary irritably. 'It's broad daylight—and why on earth should I want to steal a mess of mouldy slippers and three dirty plates that seem to be growing fungus?' She waved a hand at the bed, and then towards the ferret cage. 'Not to mention the vampire over there. I can do without her as well.'

When she saw that Jonathan's jaw no longer looked like granite, and that his mouth showed signs of relaxing, she went on quickly,' 'Besides, I don't know what you're grumbling about. Tamsin seems much better already.'

'Oh, I see,' he drawled again, still looming over her like a lion about to pounce, and with his mouth now well under control. 'And I suppose you take all the credit for that? It doesn't occur to you that I've spent hours with her every day, called in half a dozen doctors, organised round-the-clock care . . .'

'Yes, it occurs to me,' Rosemary interrupted indignantly. 'It also occurs to me that you callously refused to do the one thing she particulary asked for.'

'Oh, did I?' She saw him flex his fingers. 'And what was that, Rosemary?'

'She wanted me to visit her, of course.'

'Of course.' His face was immobile. 'And who gave you the idea she was remotely anxious to see you?'

'Does it matter? It's true, isn't it?'

'That you're irreplaceable in her affections? More important to her than her father?'

Rosemary heard the derision in his voice, and suddenly it was more than she could bear. Weeks of unhappiness, of missing this big, egotistical, confident and totally distracting man, combined in one overwhelming burst of resentment to undermine all her valiant attempts to pretend she would get over him, go on to make a happy life without him. Every good resolution she had ever made about letting him know her feelings vanished through the window in a gust of summer wind.

'No, I am not more important than her father,' she shouted at him. 'Heaven forbid that *anyone* should be more important than Jonathan Riordan. But in that warped, self-satisfied, emotionally scarred mind of yours, isn't there any room at all for . . .' she hesitated '. . . for love, and for *other* people's needs? *You* may have everything you want, the way you want it, but are you too dumb to understand that Tamsin needs more than you can give her? Or have you poisoned your brain with an over-dose of self-recrimination—because Janet died and you couldn't do anything to save her?'

Rosemary's voice, which had started fortissimo dropped slowly down to the tentative, doubtful notes of a delicate coda in andante. But she had been so caught up in her own emotional outburst that she failed to notice the effect she was having on Jonathan.

When she had started to speak, his face had been frozen and unyielding. But gradually, as her words pierced his armour, a look, first of disbelieving astonishment, and then of barely controlled rage flashed across his face.

'How dare you?' he demanded. 'How dare you accuse me of not caring about my daughter? And as for Janet—did you really expect to take her place?' The contempt in his voice was so evident that Rosemary's remaining control snapped completely.

'Damn you!' she spat, raising her arms to drum her fists furiously against his chest. 'Damn you, Jonathan Riordan!' And then, when this assault on his body produced no visible effect, she lifted her leather-clad foot and kicked him sharply in the shin.

That did produce an effect.

The derision in his eyes changed rapidly back to anger—and suddenly Rosemary found both her wrists pinioned in a hard, unyielding grip as he forced her arms behind her back and glared down into her face. She could feel his breath hot on her cheek, and the sheer force of him stirred her blood unbearably.

She tried to kick him again, but his body was too close and his thighs pressed her to the edge of Tamsin's bed. She stared up at him, mesmerised. His eyes locked into hers.

And then, slowly, something changed in their steel-grey depths. His mouth twisted, and suddenly he bent his head to press her lips in a hard, punitive kiss.

It lasted a long time. At first Rosemary tried to push away, but she found she was no match for his superior strength, bolstered as it was by the force of a flaming temper. Then gradually, as his lips compelled hers apart, and his tongue probed her mouth fiercely, her body began to respond, at first unwillingly, to the scent and feel of his maleness. And she found she no longer wanted to resist him.

He had started to kiss her as though he were wreaking vengeance, but in a very short time the feel of his firm mouth on hers became softer, and the hands grasping her wrists relaxed, and then let go entirely to move around her waist, holding her so close to him that she could hear his heartbeat. And the breath was almost crushed from her body.

With a small, incoherent cry, Rosemary flung her arms about his neck. He went on kissing her with a tenderness and longing that belied everything he had ever said about there being no future for their love, and now Rosemary was returning his kiss with all the pent-up passion of the lonely weeks without him.

Downstairs, Tamsin and Mrs Whitehead, who had been listening tensely to the sound of battle, heaved long sighs of relief and smiled complacently at each other.

'My lovely Rosemary, I've been a total fool, haven't I?' murmured Jonathan some time later. He was stroking her long hair very gently and his voice was husky and deep with—dared she believe it? Love?

She shook her head, still speechless.

I have, you know. And I should have known it the

moment I saw you protruding so enticingly from, under Tamsin's bed—because my first thought was "Thank God".' He smiled wryly. 'Then I remembered you had told me I had nothing to give you that you wanted. And to me that made a lot of sense—because for so long there was nothing I wanted to give. The truth is, I'm afraid, that that kind of thinking has been a habit with me for so many years that I thought there was no room in my life for love. Derek says he told you about Janet—and I didn't want to hurt you, Rosemary. Not the way I hurt her.' He put his hands on her shoulders and held her away from him, his grey eyes devouring every detail of her face as if he were afraid he might lose her. Then he went on slowly, 'I suppose in my heart I've always known there was no way I could have saved my wife. But I should have been with her. I wasn't, and she died. So I vowed right then and there that I'd never let another woman love me.' His mouth twisted bitterly, and all the old bleakness returned. 'That's why, when I found you here just now, and all my instincts told me to take you in my arms . . .'

'You accused me of sneaking off with three nice plates of fungus, a ferret and your daughter,' Rosemary interrupted drily.

Jonathan stared at her and, as her golden eyes gleamed up at him, the bitterness on his face changed slowly to astonishment, doubt, and finally amusement. And behind the amusement was the threat of retribution.

'Well, I had to say *something* to dispel all that self-recrimination,' she explained apologetically.

The threat became obvious and, laughing, she stepped back. But he was too quick for her, and a moment later her laughter was summarily cut off as his powerful arms crushed her against his body and her mouth was imprisoned by his lips.

'Witch,' he murmured some time later, with his big hand on the back of her neck and his face very close to hers. She smiled up at him, and he added softly, 'Is it possible that after all I do have something to give you? Can you forgive me, Rosemary? For all the accusations, and for being such a blind, obstinate fool?'

As she opened her mouth to reply, he added on a note of teasing mockery, 'And for the ferret, of course.'

Rosemary put her head on one side and regarded him solemnly. Only the light in her eyes belied the pious seriousness of her thoughtfully pursed lips. 'The ferret—certainly,' she replied judiciously. 'The accusation and pig-headedness—I'll have to think about those.'

Jonathan's eyes issued a challenge as he pulled her towards him again and kissed her long and thoroughly. 'There,' he said finally. 'Does that help you make up your mind?'

Rosemary nodded, breathlessly, and lifted her arm to run her fingers softly over the hard planes of his face, smoothing the lines of strain around his eyes. 'There's nothing to forgive.' She smiled. 'Well—not much. I didn't understand—how Janet died. I thought you were just using her as an excuse to avoid involvement.'

'Perhaps I was, partly,' he agreed, the laughter dying from his eyes. 'I loved Janet, of course. But it was a young man's love and I took more than I gave. For a while after she died I was too stunned—and too busy trying to get to know my own daughter—to worry much about women. When I did think about them, I decided that all I needed was physical satisfaction. I had no problem finding that—and if any woman wanted more, she was out of my life like a shot. Then I met you. And my complacency was shattered for ever. Life wasn't so simple any more.'

'I know,' agreed Rosemary. 'You were an unwanted complication in my life too, so perhaps I should have understood. I should never have accused you of only pretending to love Janet. Or of not caring about Tamsin. Can you forgive *me*?'

He gave an exclamation that was more like a groan and held her against his chest. 'Of course I can. I knew even then, when I wanted to murder you, that you were only reacting to the hurt I'd inflicted on you.' He pressed his lips against her forehead, and added drily, 'Especially when you objected to my lampshade—which as a matter of fact I'm not too fond of myself.'

Rosemary lifted her head and gave him a doubtful smile. 'Really? And I suppose you were just too lazy to change it.'

'Right,' he said softly. 'Slothful to the end, that's me.'

'Hmm,' murmured Rosemary disbelievingly. 'There wasn't much sloth about you that night when Tamsin was communing with Colin behind the cabin.'

'No, but that was different. I'd been dying of frustration and need for you all day. Something exploded in me then. I wanted to make love to you desperately, you know. But I didn't want you to love me.'

'So you solved the problem by losing your temper.' She slid her fingers slowly through his hair.

'Witch,' he said again, moving his hand in slow, tantalising circles at the bottom of her spine. 'But you're right, of course. And of course it didn't solve anything—because I didn't have everything I wanted, the way I wanted it, as you so inaccurately put it. I didn't have you, Rosemary. And after we got back from that memorable field trip, the gap in my life was brought home to me with a vengeance. I wanted you like hell—but I was determined I wouldn't have you—even if you'd let me, which I doubted.'

'I know. Tamsin said you were wandering around the house like the Ghost of Christmas Yet to Come.'

'Did she now? I'll have to have a word with that young lady.'

Rosemary looked up quickly, afraid she had got Tamsin into trouble. But Jonathan was smiling.

'And then I decided to drown my sorrows with Deloraine, realised I didn't want to after all, came home in a foul mood and tripped over the table. When I woke up, there you were, an angel of mercy bending over me. It was like a dream come true. Only, the dream ended, and I woke up.'

'Don't I know it! You were a beast.'

'I wasn't.' He grinned. 'I was just a mildly drunk, sex-starved man who thought the gods had finally seen fit to reward me.'

'Reward you?' exclaimed Rosemary, her eyes widening in taunting disbelief. 'Reward you for what, for heaven's sake?'

'For having the good sense to fall in love with the loveliest woman in the world.'

Rosemary closed her eyes. He had said it at last and she was so happy she wanted to laugh out loud. Until she remembered he hadn't mentioned marriage. Then she wanted to cry.

'If you were in love with me,' she said carefully, 'why wouldn't you even let me see Tamsin?'

He shook his head. 'Blind obstinacy again, damn foolishness—habit—you name it. But I almost gave in when you phoned that time. I desperately wanted to. But I suppose, in my arrogance, I thought Tamsin and I could manage without you—that in the long run we'd all be better off.'

Rosemary twisted a button on his shirt, her fingers feeling the smooth cloth and the hardness of his chest beneath. 'And now?' she whispered. 'Has anything really happened to change things, Jonathan?'

With a sound that was half-groan, half laugh, he pulled her to him, wrapping his arms tightly around her back and rocking her against his chest. 'Yes,' he said, in that warm, deep voice that sent shivers up her spine. 'Yes, something's happened. You happened. When I started to kiss you just now, because you kicked me and because I couldn't stop myself, I thought it would be for the last time. But then I knew—I knew I couldn't bear that. I don't want any last times for us, Rosemary. I don't want to spend the rest of my life without you—although it's no more than I deserve.'

He held her away from him and took her hands firmly in his own.

'Will you marry me, Rosemary Reid?' he asked quietly. 'As warped, self-satisfied and emotionally scarred as I am?'

Rosemary looked up into deep grey eyes that were no longer cold and remote, but filled with warmth and tenderness—for her. She saw love and hope and hunger. She even saw his heart beating beneath his shirt. But she couldn't see the agonising effort it cost him to hide the uncertainty in that heart—an uncertainty which none of their earlier banter had done anything to diminish—and to summon the strength to accept her answer. Whatever it might be.

'Did I really say all those things?' asked Rosemary, smiling softly. 'I didn't mean them.' Her face alight with love, she gave a long sigh of happiness and added solemnly, 'Yes, I'll marry you, Jonathan Riordan. I couldn't marry anybody else.'

From the doorwary behind them there was a sudden loud burst of applause at two cheering figures erupted instantly into the room.

'Congratulations!' shouted a misty-eyed Mrs Whitehead. 'That's the best news I've heard in a year.'

'Oh, Dad!' cried Tamsin, throwing her arms around her father. 'It's the best news *I've* heard in my life.'


Jonathan and Rosemary were married three days later by special licence, in a quiet double ceremony with Derek and Bozo.

At first Jonathan had hesitated to suggest a wedding that would not be exclusively Rosemary's, but when he tentatively broached Derek's idea that it might add to the happiness of the occasion if both principals of Riordan and Maloney were united in marriage on the same day, Rosemary was delighted.

'It's a wonderful idea,' she said happily, her fingers prodding at a suspicious green blob in the door of Jonathan's fridge.

'Good. What on earth do you think you're doing?'

'Looking for eggs.'

'There aren't any.'

'There never are,' muttered Tamsin from behind him.

'Stop complaining, young lady.' Jonathan ruffled her hair. 'Things are about to change.'

'They are for Uncle Derek, too,' remarked Tamsin. 'I can't wait to meet Aunt Bozo.'

Rosemary couldn't either. She had envisaged a large, Amazonian woman with a hearty laugh, a loud, carrying voice and a rucksack and binoculars permanently strapped to her back.

But when, the night before the wedding, the two couples met for a quiet meal at a small Japanese restaurant near English Bay, Rosemary was amazed to be introduced to a small, fragile-looking pixie with merry black eyes and a soft, musical voice. It was easy to understand why Derek had fallen in love.

When Rosemary opened her eyes on the morning of her wedding, the sun was already shining through her bedroom window. A good omen. It was going to be hot and bright. Too hot for a wedding, perhaps, but she didn't mind a bit.

For the last time, she slammed toast into her toaster and made just enough for one. After today, she and Jonathan would be eating breakfast together. But not in Bangladesh. She smiled, as she remembered Derek's hopeful suggestion that they should share the honeymoon, as well as the wedding. But Jonathan had been adamant about that. He insisted that Venice was the only possible place for lovers, and with a burst of energy which left Rosemary gasping he had arranged flights, tickets and accommodation with the speed and competence of a newly repaired computer. Alice, who had a healthy interest in the well-being of her shares, had promised to keep an eye on the business in Derek and Jonathan's absense.

I'll miss having Alice as a neighbour—and Murphy and Muffin— thought Rosemary as breakfast over, she waited for Tamsin, who was to be her bridesmaid. On the other hand, she would gain Mrs Whitehead and her brood, which Jonathan said was an experience not to be missed.

A short time later Henry delivered Tamsin, and a little while after that Rosemary's parents arrived from

Kelowna, both looking slightly stunned at the sudden announcement of their daughter's marriage. To their great regret, Jonathan's family had not been able to come at such short notice.

The ceremony took place in the flower-decked living-room of a lovely old house near Spanish Banks, belonging to Bozo's aunt.

Jonathan felt his throat contract as Rosemary walked towards him, looking as serene and beautiful as he had ever seen her in her pale gold, calf-length dress with the lace-trimmed bodice and soft, draped panels of pleated chiffon. When the smiling company watching them saw the look he bestowed on his bride, a number of hands rose quickly to brush away surreptitious tears.

Afterwards, the two couples and their guests gathered for a small, informal reception, and Tamsin, who looked suddenly slimmer and more grown-up in her high heels and demurely fitted blue dress, came laughing up to her new stepmother with Bozo's niece in tow.

'Judy says Dad got the best of the bargain,' she announced, indicating Bozo's blushing young bridemaid.

'Does she? Why's that?' asked Rosemary, glancing radiantly up at her husband and feeling quite sure that she had the best of all bargains herself.

'Because you're prettier than he is, giggled Tamsin.

'Well, I should hope so,' said Jonathan, putting an arm around his bride and smiling down at her.

But what he was really thinking was that in that ethereal gold dress, and with the wonderful soft glow in her eyes, Rosemary looked more than just pretty. She was lovelier than a dream. The dream he had almost lost.

All around them their guests jostled and laughed. Rosemary's parents no longer looked stunned, but relieved and happy that their daughter had found a man they could like and approve of—and whom she obviously adored.

Over in a corner, Aunt Alice was talking to Bozo, and she looked as satisfactorily won over as Derek could possibly have hoped—won over and utterly flabbergasted that this dainty, sloe-eyed flower could be the dreaded Bozo of her imaginings.

Rosemary also saw Henry, standing with his mother against a panelled wall. He was wielding a champagne bottle with enthusiasm, and looking more cheerful than ever.

'I expect he's thanking his stars that it's you stuck with me and not him,' she remarked laughing to her husband.

'Then he doesn't know what he's missing,' said Jonathan, gazing thoughtfully at the ceiling. 'Iguanas, gerbils, rats, fish . . .'

'Not to mention Dracula,' put in Rosemary caustically. 'I'm not the only one with a predilection for hazardous fauna. And on top of that I have sky-diving to contend with.'

'What makes you think that?'

'Tamsin.'

'Ah. The usual source of information leaks. Does it worry you, Rosemary?'

'It does a little,' she confessed.

'Then I'll stick to more stimulating passion for a while.' He smiled at her, a curving, sensuous smile, and Rosemary swallowed quickly. 'Come on, beloved,' he suggested. 'Let's get out of here for a minute. It's a beautiful summer, afternoon, I can smell the sea in the air—and I want to be alone with my bride.'

Rosemary looked around the room. Their guests were all talking and laughing and enjoying themselves, especially the Whitehead men, who were carrying on an animated and throughly unromantic discussion about tomorrow's football game.

'All right,' she agreed, after checking her guests again. 'They'll never even notice we've gone.'

Outside the sun was beating down, and Jonathan led Rosemary across the bright green lawns to a rustic wooden bench beneath a small grove of fir trees. In the distance, the tall buildings of Vancouver gleamed sharply white against the sky, and closer to hand myriad white and coloured sails dotted the waters of the inlet.

Jonathan sat down and pulled Rosemary on to his knees. 'Well, Mrs Riordan, how does it feel?' he asked.

For answer, Rosemary wrapped her arms around his neck and bent her lips to his. 'Like this,' she whispered.

Several minutes later, as Jonathan started to let her go because he said he needed a breathing break, there was a sudden deafening uproar from inside the house, followed by Mrs Whitehead's ringing tones telling someone to behave himself—or else.

'Or else what, I wonder?' murmured Rosemary, rubbing her cheek along the top of Jonathan's forehead. 'She doesn't sound as though she means it.'

'No,' agreed Jonathan, as he gently stroked her back. 'I have every admiration for Mrs Whitehead. She's put up with Jack Whitehead and those five appalling sons of hers for over twenty-five years—and she's still smiling.'

'Mm,' agreed Rosemary. 'It's an achievement, all right.' She stood up reluctantly and turned towards the house. 'We'd better be getting back, I suppose. You know I don't think I could manage five sons—even though I do teach kids all day. Maybe *because* I do.'

Jonathan caught her arm and pulled her round to face

him. 'A terrifying prospect, indeed,' he agreed lazily. Then he looked into her eyes and asked, suddenly serious, 'Do you want children, Rosemary? I never asked—because *I* wanted you.'

'Yes,' said Rosemary simply. 'But not five Whitehead clones.' She put her head on one side. 'A boy and a girl, I think—and Tamsin, of course.'

'Suits me,' replied Jonathan. He ran his eyes suggestively over her figure. 'Shall we start on them now?'

'Lovely idea,' nodded Rosemary, taking a quick step away from him. 'But I don't think . . .' She glanced pointedly towards the house and, as he stretched out his hand, took another step back and promptly fell over a rockery.

Jonathan shook his head as he reached down to pull her to her feet. 'From elegant bride to mud-spattered ragamuffin at a stroke,' he murmured as his hands brushed dirt and grass clippings from her skirt.

'I'm not a rag . . .' began Rosemary. But then Jonathan stopped brushing as he felt the soft thighs beneath her dress. His arm encircled her waist and her words ended in a little, choking sigh.

He pulled her close against him.

In the end, a good many minutes had passed before he released her again, and the two of them walked hand in hand towards the house.

'Those babies you mentioned,' said Jonathan, as the sounds of laughter from inside drew nearer. 'Won't you mind taking time off to have them? I'll never forget how you went up one side of me and down the other when I told you you were too young to cope with Tamsin. Your job means a lot to you, doesn't it?'

'Yes, it does.' Rosemary looked up at her husband,

standing tall and imposing in the dark suit which moulded his figure to perfection. As usual, she felt her heart jump against her ribs. Then she smiled mischievously. 'It does mean a lot to me,' she agreed, 'but of course after teaching one student who grew up to be a murderer, two house-breakers, a forger—a very bright lad, that one—and a nice case of assault with a deadly weapon, I feel I've made my contribution to education. I'm quite looking forward to a few years off with a couple of relatively law-abiding babies.'

Jonathan's dark eyebrows had risen as Rosemary, with a primly straight face, catalogued her successes. Then his lips twitched, and he stopped walking and caught her around her waist.

'I underestimated your talents, my love,' he said softly, running his fingers slowly up her spine.

'Maybe you did,' smiled Rosemary. She rested her cheek blissfully against his shoulder. 'You said I taught biology and groping . . .'

'And love and laughter and how to drive a man to madness . . .'

'And you've a lifetime ahead of you to find out about the rest.'

'That's what I'm afraid of,' groaned Jonathan. But he was smiling when he said it, and as Rosemary laughed up at him he added, 'But if you want the truth, my darling, that's why I can hardly wait.'

# HARLEQUIN
## *Romance*

## Coming Next Month

**#3019 THE SNOW GARDEN Bethany Campbell**
Hedy Hansen needs to ignore Christmas and the painful memories the season brings. But she hasn't reckoned with her new Holly Street neighbors, especially the irrepressible Ty Marek.

**#3020 FOLLY TO LOVE Lynn Jacobs**
Ross Courtenay always comes along at the right time—and Olivia has never needed his helping hand more than now. But can she just close her eyes and let him take over her life—especially after he's admitted his dishonorable intentions?

**#3021 LETTERS OF LOVE Judy Kaye**
Too many letters are complicating Kate Matthew's life. There's her correspondence with the mysterious C.G. of Chicago, and her letters about nurses' rights to Dr. Chase Kincaid, her boss at St. Mike's Hospital in Fargo. And then, there are the love letters written by Chase—to his ex-wife.

**#3022 RIDDELL OF RIVERMOON Miriam MacGregor**
Ten years after her mother and aunt had parted in anger, Fleur, at Luke Riddell's request, comes to Rivermoon to help her Aunt Jessica. Only hoping to end the family feud, Fleur can't understand why Luke should mistrust her motives.

**#3023 LET ME COUNT THE WAYS Leigh Michaels**
Sara Prentiss has found a haven in New England's Chandler College and in Olivia Reynolds, the mother she's longed for. Then famous thriller writer Adam Merrill arrives—and finds a mystery right in the middle of Sara's peaceful little world!

**#3024 THE FATEFUL BARGAIN Betty Neels**
Sebastian van Tecqx provides the solution to Emily's most pressing problem—in return for her temporary help with his convalescent sister in Delft. Emily knows it's hopeless, but with Sebastian's constant presence, she can't stop herself falling in love.

Available in December wherever paperback books are sold, or through Harlequin Reader Service:

In the U.S.
901 Fuhrmann Blvd.
P.O. Box 1397
Buffalo, N.Y. 14240-1397

In Canada
P.O. Box 603
Fort Erie, Ontario
L2A 5X3

# HARLEQUIN'S "BIG WIN"
## SWEEPSTAKES RULES & REGULATIONS
### NO PURCHASE NECESSARY TO ENTER OR RECEIVE A PRIZE

1. To enter and join the Harlequin Reader Service, scratch off the pink metallic strips on all your BIG WIN tickets #1-#6. This will reveal the values for each sweepstakes entry number, the number of free books you will receive and your free bonus gift as part of our Reader Service. If you do not wish to take advantage of our introduction to the Harlequin Reader Service but wish to enter the Sweepstakes only, scratch off the pink metallic strips on your BIG WIN tickets #1-#4 only. To enter, return your entire sheet of tickets intact. Incomplete and/or inaccurate entries are not eligible for that section or section(s) of prizes. Not responsible for mutilated or unreadable entries or inadvertent printing errors. Mechanically reproduced entries are null and void.

2. Either way your unique Sweepstakes numbers will be compared against the list of winning numbers generated at random by the computer. In the event that all prizes are not claimed, random drawings will be held from all entries received from all presentations to award all unclaimed prizes. All cash prizes are payable in U.S. funds. This is in addition to any free, surprise or mystery gifts that might be offered. The following prizes are awarded in this sweepstakes: *Grand Prize (1) $1,000,000; First Prize (1) $35,000; Second Prize (1) $10,000; Third Prize (3) $5,000; Fourth Prize (10) $1,000; Fifth Prize (25) $500; Sixth Prize (5000)$5.

   *This Sweepstakes contains a Grand Prize offering of a $1,000,000 annuity. Winner may elect to receive $25,000 a year for 40 years without interest totalling $1,000,000 or $350,000 in one cash payment. Entrants may cancel Reader Service at any time without cost or obligation to buy (see details in center insert card).

3. Extra Bonus Prize: This presentation offers two extra bonus prizes valued at $30,000 each to be awarded in a random drawing from all entries received.

4. Versions of this Sweepstakes with different graphics will be offered in other mailings or at retail outlets by Torstar Corp. and its affiliates. This promotion is being conducted under the supervision of Marden-Kane, Inc., an independent judging organization. By entering this Sweepstakes, each entrant accepts and agrees to be bound by these rules and the decisions of the judges, which shall be final and binding. Odds of winning in the random drawing are dependent upon the total number of entries received. Taxes, if any, are the sole responsibility of the winners. Prizes are non-transferable. All entries must be received by March 31, 1990. The drawing will take place on or about April 30, 1990 at the offices of Marden-Kane, Inc., Lake Success, NY.

5. This offer is open to residents of the U.S., the United Kingdom and Canada, 18 years or older except employees of Torstar Corp., its affiliates, subsidiaries, Marden-Kane, Inc. and all other agencies and persons connected with conducting this Sweepstakes. All Federal, State and local laws apply. Void wherever prohibited or restricted by law.

6. Winners will be notified by mail and may be required to execute an affidavit of eligibility and release that must be returned within 14 days after notification. Canadian winners will be required to answer a skill-testing question. Winners consent to the use of their name, photograph and/or likeness for advertising and publicity in conjunction with this and similar promotions without additional compensation.

7. For a list of our most current major prize winners, send a stamped, self-addressed envelope to: WINNERS LIST c/o MARDEN-KANE, INC., P.O. BOX 701, SAYREVILLE, NJ 08871.

If Sweepstakes entry form is missing, please print your name and address on a 3" × 5" piece of plain paper and send to:

| In the U.S. | In Canada |
|---|---|
| Harlequin's "BIG WIN" Sweepstakes | Harlequin's "BIG WIN" Sweepstakes |
| 901 Fuhrmann Blvd. | P.O. Box 609 |
| Box 1867 | Fort Erie, Ontario |
| Buffalo, NY 14269-1867 | L2A 5X3 |

LTY-H119

Wonderful, luxurious gifts can be yours with proofs-of-purchase from any specially marked "Indulge A Little" Harlequin or Silhouette book with the Offer Certificate properly completed, plus a check or money order (do not send cash) to cover postage and handling payable to Harlequin/Silhouette "Indulge A Little, Give A Lot" Offer. We will send you the specified gift.

**Mail-in-Offer**

| | OFFER CERTIFICATE | | | |
|---|---|---|---|---|
| Item: | A. Collector's Doll | B. Soaps in a Basket | C. Potpourri Sachet | D. Scented Hangers |
| # of Proofs-of-Purchase | 18 | 12 | 6 | 4 |
| Postage & Handling | $3.25 | $2.75 | $2.25 | $2.00 |
| Check One | | | | |

Name _____

Address _____ Apt. # _____

City _____ State _____ Zip _____

ONE PROOF OF PURCHASE

To collect your free gift by mail you must include the necessary number of proofs-of-purchase plus postage and handling with offer certificate.

HR-2

Harlequin®/Silhouette

Mail this certificate, designated number of proofs-of-purchase and check or money order for postage and handling to:

**INDULGE A LITTLE**
**P.O. Box 9055**
**Buffalo, N.Y. 14269-9055**